WANDLORE

Power and Practice

A Complete Guide to the Wizard Wand

Principles of Wizardry – Volume One

Also by Annette M Musta

The Caledon Crystal

Principles of Wizardry – Volume Two

The Wizard's Cookbook

To order these books, please visit our website at:

www.arhbooks.com

To Order any of the Wands you have seen in this book, please visit The Wandmaker's website at:

www.thewandshop.com

WANDLORE

Power and Practice

A Complete Guide to the Wizard Wand

Principles of Wizardry – Volume One

by

The Wandmaker and Annette M Musta

WANDLORE

Power and Practice
A Complete Guide to the Wizard Wand
Principles of Wizardry - Volume One

Published by ARH Books – Venetia PA
ARH Books and the logo are trademarks of ARH Books

ISBN: 978-0-9798639- 3 - 6 Softcover

First Edition, First Printing December 14, 2007
This book was printed in the United States of America

To order additional copies of this book, or any other ARH Books publication, contact:

ARH BOOKS
www.arhbooks.com

DEDICATION

To Aemilia, Aaron, and Russell – May your futures be filled with happiness and magic

CONTENTS

WANDLORE

Power and Practice

A Complete Guide to the Wizard Wand

Principles of Wizardry – Volume One

WANDLORE

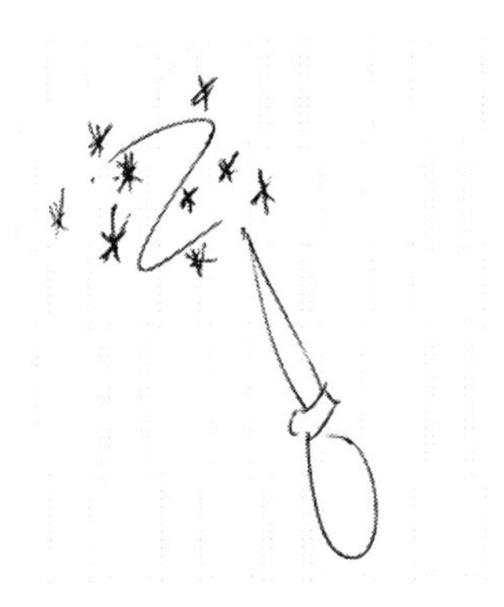

The Wizard Wand ...

... is a wizard's single most important instrument, yet it is more than a mere symbol. The wand is an extension of the wizard, part of the wizard, one with the wizard. It is a weapon and a defense. It can conjure objects, cast spells, and transfigure. It can protect life and it can kill. In the hands of a wizard, a wand is pure power.

Every young wizard dreams of their first wand. You remember how it was. The long wait through childhood, often using an older sibling's cast-off or even plain sticks for

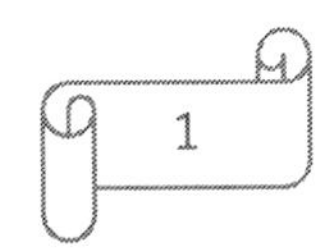

a wand, the build-up to the day when you will finally come of wand age, and then, at long last, it is time. Your parents join you on this special day. You tentatively step through the door to the Wand Shop. The Wandmaker takes your measurements and sizes you up. Then it happens, you pick up the wand destined to be your wand, you feel the tingle run up your fingers, through your arm, and straight into your heart. You have found your partner, your one true companion who will join you on every adventure, cast every spell you ask of it. You have found your Wand.

Even among the non-magical (called humans in this book, wizards are wizards), the wand is legendary. Wands often appear in human literature, wielded by wizards, and at times, humans. The wand is a symbol of power and a mysterious magic. The human world's inaccurate portrayal of the wand (and the wizard) is highly amusing but many humans desire a wand believing it will give them magical powers. (Of course it does not work this way but humans still buy wands.)

What is it about a basic stick that has captured the imagination of so many?

WANDLORE

The answer is simple and complex for the wand is both the symbol of the wizard and the wizard's most important tool. A wandless wizard still has power (and a select few are just as powerful without a wand, but this is a rare gift indeed) but the wizard cannot channel that power. Try casting the simplest spell without a wand. The spell may work but it will often be weak, non-binding, or fail altogether. Cast the same spell with your wand and you have true magic.

Wand styles and materials differ across the world. Yet one aspect of the wand remains the same. This is the secret that stumps so many humans, something they do not seem to understand. *There is no such thing as a magic wand*. The wand itself is NOT "magical". It cannot give power where power is not already present. The wand is the instrument, a tool used by the wizard to channel their power or, to use another term, their magic. In fact, the wand is merely the instrument. The magic comes from the wizard.

That is not to say the wand is unimportant. The wand and the wizard share a special and unique symbiotic relationship. Once they are bonded, they grow together in power and ability. The wand, in essence, becomes a part of the wizard. The wizard, in turn, leaves their own mark on their wand. While the wand remains an inert object, unable to exert its will or act on its own without its wizard (though this point is contended by the Killarney theory, discussed later in this book), it can absorb powers from its wizard. Wandmakers believe a wand can recognize its owner. If another wizard attempts to use the wand, it will often react to this intrusion by refusing to cast spells, casting weak spells, or even reflecting the spell back on the wizard who tried to use it.

Wandmakers have long studied the phenomenon that is the Wand. This extensive knowledge has been applied to create superior wands. Unfortunately, in this day and age, anyone who can carve wood thinks they can be a wandmaker. This has resulted in the appearance of the many sub-standard, mass produced wands that are on the market today. As all wizards know, these wands are fakes, unable to produce even the weakest spell.

A true Wandmaker has studied their craft. A true Wandmaker hones their skills over many years, gaining in knowledge and ability. A true Wandmaker knows a wand is more than a mere stick. A true Wandmaker creates true

WANDLORE

wands.

I am one of those Wandmakers. For the first time ever, the ISW® (International Society of Wandmakers®) has authorized the publication of some of the secrets known only to its members. We have done so in the hope that wizards (and humans) will acquire the knowledge to separate the asli from the jutha (true wands from the substandard, false wands).

This book is a primer of the history and creation of the wizard's most important tool – the Wand. It covers the history of the wand, the creation of a fine wand, the wand-wizard bond, the elements of the wand, and wands around the world. I have also included numerous pictures of wands. (A word to all of you humans or underage wizards reading this book, there are no spells in this book. If you are looking for spells, I suggest you find a good basic spellbook at your local Wizard Book Shop.)

Happy reading and have a magical day.

The Wandmaker

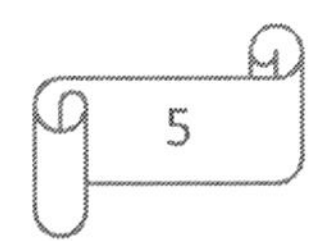

PRINCIPLES OF WIZARDRY
VOLUME ONE

CHAPTER ONE

The History of the Wand and Wandmaking

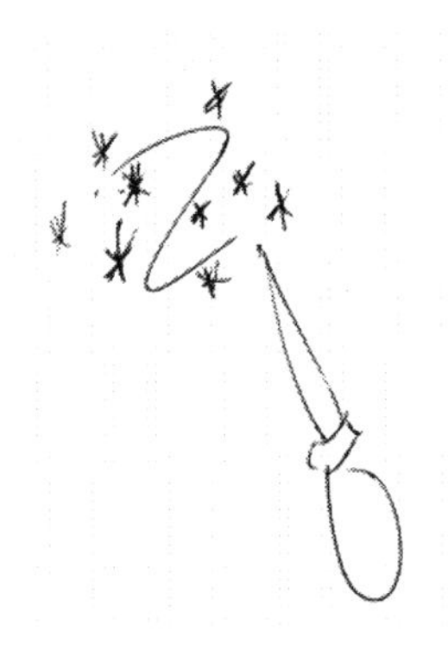

Wandmaking is an ancient craft dating back at least 12,000 years. (The history of the wand is closely tied to the history of the wizard however wizard history is too complex to be covered here in full. In this book, we shall only mention the parts of wizard history that relate directly to the history of the wand and wandmaking.) The original Wandmakers were the elves,

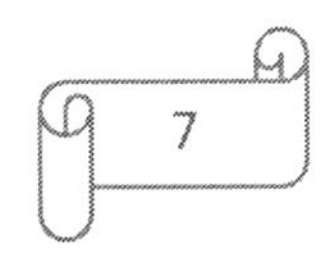

who crafted their wands for the use of the wizards at the time (different in origin from modern-day wizards). The rise of modern wizards, which coincided with the rise of the humans, shifted the focus of wandmaking to wizards but the lore and the crafting of wands was passed down from the ancient elven Wandmakers to wizard Wandmakers practicing their art to this day.

Ancient Wands

The first known wands, as mentioned above, were created by elves. The elves, of course, were the first established magical society in documented history. Ancient elves, much like elves today, had the ability to manipulate natural substances to enhance the magical capabilities of the substance. A lot of the modern wizard's weapons and armor comes from materials originally invented by the elves thousands of years ago.

The ancient elves used their knowledge to create the very first wands. By all accounts, these wands were exquisitely crafted creations the likes of which today's modern Wandmakers can only aspire to. The wands were crafted from wood, elvish metals and jewels, and elvish ivory (not to be confused with the human ivory of today – elvish ivory was a created substance and it did not come from the tusks of elephants, which did not exist at the time). The wands ranged in size from the modern handheld wands (approximately fourteen to twenty-four inches) to full-size staves.

Ancient elves (like the modern elves), did not use wands. (Elves are one of the magical species who do not need a wand to channel their power but they also do not cast spells.) It seems the earliest elven Wandmakers created wands simply for the knowledge and the pleasure. Elves are naturally curious and, due to their immortality, constantly seeking ways to increase their own knowledge.

None of these earliest elven wands exist today. We do have some idea of what they looked like from copies of ancient paintings which were once in the great elven havens. These wands were intricately carved, crafted from wood or elvish metals and sometimes heavily studded with jewels. Modern Wandmakers have tried to recreate these wands and while they can make the wands look right, only elven Wandmakers can actually make these wands properly.

We are fortunate to have several of these re-created wands to study and admire (though it is doubtful that these re-created wands are as powerful as the originals).

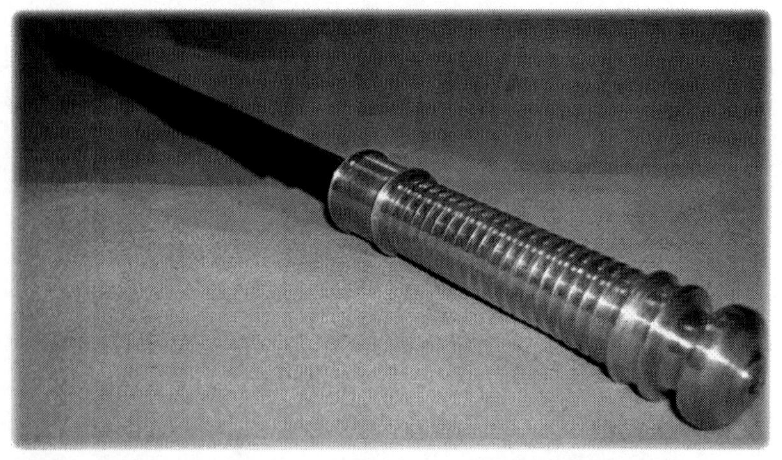

This is a recreation of an ancient elvish wand crafted by VirgiFingal of the Salien. The wood is Coeden. The handle is adimeta. In ancient times, this wand would have been studded with jewels.

At some point, believed to be about around 11,000 BCE (BCE means Before the Common Era. Human dates are given in this book as this is the most commonly accepted way of marking time throughout the world.), the first wizards appeared. The details of the lives and activities of these wizards have been lost in the mists of time. The accounts we have indicate these wizards were not exactly of human origin, nor were they elves. They seem to be their own sub-species. Their numbers never were great and they lived among the peoples of the time.

While little is known of the actions of these wizards, their close relationship with the elves is well documented. It was the elves who made wands for these wizards. At first, these wands were of the standard length. But the wizards seem to have preferred longer wands which were in fact staves. (For modern wizards who may not know, staves are very large wands approximately the size of the wizard, around five or six feet.) The wizards used their staves much like modern wizards use their wands – as a method to channel their power.

None of the original staves has survived the long march of time. However, elven drawings of these staves exist in one or two of the libraries in the great magical realms and have been recreated by modern wandmakers.

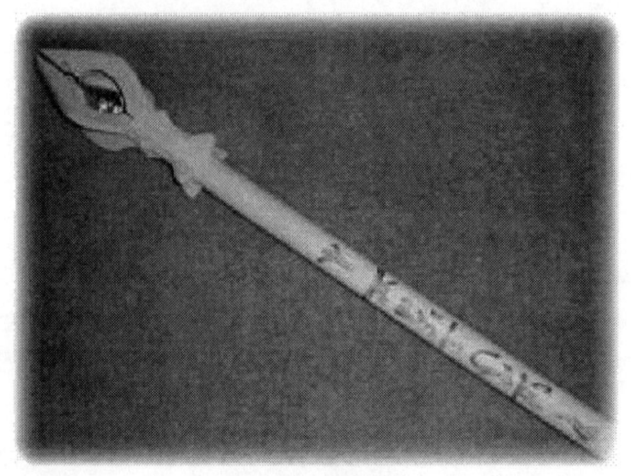

This is a recreation of a stave made by the elves for the ancient wizards. It was crafted by VirgiFingal of the Salien. Note the crystal in the top of the stave.

The ancient society of wizards disappears around the same time as human-derived wizards appear. Some elven histories imply the ancient wizards imparted their powers on a line of human kings and their descendents (one story claims this line was descended from both the elves and an extremely ancient line of humans who in turn were descended from the elves). In any case, the ancient wizards disappeared and the human wizards, the descendents of which live to this day (the Salien, Galdorgalere, Astrals, and most likely the Sabedora all come from this line of wizards), came into power.

WANDLORE

The human wizards (from this point on referred to simply as wizards) also enjoyed a close friendship with the remaining elves. The elves continued to provide arms, armor, and most importantly wands for these wizards. Unlike their predecessors, the wizards used wands as they are known today. These wands were often longer in length than modern wands (twenty to thirty inches). Some histories claim these early wizards were much taller than modern wizards and attribute the exceptionally long length of their wands to their height.

Elven wands were finely crafted, durable, and probably the best wands ever made. Elves always based their wands on wood, for wood has the purest magical powers. Elves never used parts of magical creatures in their wands (like phoenix feathers, dragon whiskers, and the other inserts that are popular in some parts of the world today). The elves did use two materials that can only be described as "metal-like substances". These substances were elven creations, much like the adimeta of today. The metals were usually used in the handles while the wand itself was of wood. The handles were often embedded with jewels. The surviving documents do not say if the jewels were simply for decoration or if they enhanced the power of the wand.

There is only one surviving wand from this era. It is the *Virga de Aba* (the Wand of Life), held by the Salien (the Realm of Wizards who live in North America). Few wizards have ever seen this wand as it is a treasure beyond compare and well protected by the Salien. I have been lucky enough to be one of the chosen few. I have held this wand and have had the opportunity to study it. It is truly a wonder. It is heavy by today's standards. The wand is of a red wood (most likely an ancestor of bloodwood). The handle is a gold elven metal. It is set with red, blue, green, black, and clear jewels (elven creations far greater than today's rubies, sapphires, emeralds, onyx, and diamonds).

You can feel the power radiating from the wand even as you approach it. It is imbued with powers from every wizard who has used it. This wand is the wand of the Salien royal family, whose powers are legendary. As we know, this family has given us some of the greatest wizards of all time. As a Wandmaker, I have created and handled thousands of wands but the *Virga de Aba* is the pinnacle of wand creation. It is the most powerful and the most beautiful wand I have ever seen. It is pure perfection.

As you can imagine, the Salien do not allow this wand to be seen by many, certainly not by humans and wizards who may be reading this book. However, they did allow me to make a recreation of the *Virga de Aba*. Of course I had to use modern elements. For this wand I used bloodwood with a gold handle. I set the handle with precious stones (onyx, diamonds, sapphires, emeralds, and rubies). My re-creation looks very similar to the Wand of Life however it does not have the power or feel of the original.

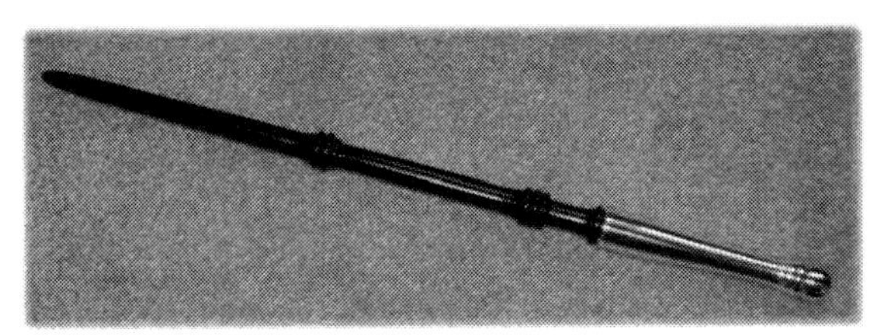

This is my recreation of the Virga de Aba.

The elder wizards, as mentioned, depended on elves for their wands. However, as the years went on and more and more elves departed for the elven havens, the task of wandmaking fell to the wizards themselves. These early wizard Wandmakers studied with the elves, learning their craft at the hands of the greatest Wandmakers of all time. These early wizard wands resembled elven wands in many ways. They were based on wood, often with heavier handles, sometimes made of metal. These wands had intricately carved handles with jewels and crystals embedded in the designs. The wands appeared delicate, almost fragile, but were very strong and durable.

As wizarding societies grew and flourished, the demand for wands and wandmakers increased. Wizard Wandmakers met most of this demand but it was during this time period (around 8000 BCE) that the most interesting period of wandmaking occurred. This was the era of the goblin-made wands.

Elven society declined during this period. Many elves departed for the havens or migrated to other areas. (It is believed the rise of humans and wizards made the elves feel crowded. Whatever the case, elven enclaves became fewer and much less populated.) Wizard settlements grew in size. One of these abutted the largest of the goblin enclaves. The goblins had been peaceful for over a thousand years by this point. They had developed a close relationship with the remaining elves, who are believed to be their kin. (For a complete history of the goblins, please read *Wizards and Magic, A Comprehensive History – Principles of Wizardry Volume Four.)* The elves taught the goblins their various crafts and by all accounts goblin armor far surpassed elven armor (which was the best armor of its time).

Goblins soon delved into the realm of wandmaking. Most of the goblin wands were for the goblins who (though immortal) do cast offensive and defensive spells. A few goblin wands made their way into the hands of the local wizards. Soon goblin-made wands became extremely popular, especially among wizard warriors. Heavier than wizard wands, goblin wands of this time often used metals for the handles. Strong with fighting spells, goblin wands were perfect for the era as wizards often had to fight off roving bands of fallen wizards, trolls, giants, various beasts, and even some ruthless humans. (It was not illegal at the time to use magic in front of or against humans.) Goblin wands were also extremely durable. Wizards of the time often had two or more wands - wood wands made by other wizards for everyday use and their goblin made wands that they took into battle.

While these ancient goblin-made wands no longer

exist, goblins continue to make wands for their own purposes. Goblin-made wands are favored by goblins and goblins often make the wands (really large staves) for modern giants. The ISW welcomed all goblin Wandmakers when it was formed. There is a significant number of goblin Wandmakers registered with the ISW today. Most are located in North America and Europe, where the majority of the goblins live.

Around 5500 BCE, the wizard communities of the old world, crowded out by the increasing population of humans, departed on The Exodus for the *Ocidenia Expona* (the "Lands of the Far West" now called the Americas by humans). This vast new country was originally discovered by the elves during their travels. At the time of The Exodus, there were several small elven settlements in Ocidenia Expona. The land was also the home of native wizards, called *Mellas de eo Riena* (literally "natives of the land") by the newcomers. The Mellas de eo Riena had highly developed and sophisticated communities. Recognizing the needs of the Exiles, the Mellas granted large areas of land to the Exiles. The two communities lived in peace and often intermarried leading to the merging of the Mellas and the Exiles (now called the Salien) into large, diverse settlements.

WANDLORE

The Mellas de eo Riena had their own style of wands. Mellas wands were thick and tapered down to the bottom. The wands were two to three feet long (they were not wands at all but small staves). The Mellas staves were wrapped with vines, flowers, and leaves and then sealed or finished so the wrappings fused with the wands. The Mellas believed these additions brought the spirit of the elements into the stave, thereby increasing its power.

Salien Wandmakers incorporated the concept of wrapping into their own wands. Salien wands from this era often had thick, heavy handles (reminiscent of the goblin-made wands), though some Salien wands were handleless in the style of the Mellas. Crystals and jewels were still embedded in the intricately carved handles while the wands were wrapped with natural elements. Modern Wandmakers consider the wands of this era to be very "busy" with far too many elements. Indeed, modern Wandmakers refuse to incorporate so many elements into their wands as they believe the elements often "fight" each other and weaken the powers of the wand.

This is a wrapped Salien wand circa 5300 BCE. Note the Mellas-style wrappings and the lack of a handle.

As the Salien became settled in their new home and prior to the War of the Three Powers, some Salien joined with the Wandering Elves and explored the world. This was known as The Great Journey and led the Magical Peoples of the West to discover other Wizard Realms around the world.

WANDLORE

History of Wandmaking Around the Globe

Magical societies came into being around 7800 BCE in the area now known as Asia. Prior to this time, there are no surviving records to indicate there were wizards in any place other than the old world (modern Europe). It is not known if these "new" realms of wizards were migrants or if they developed from the peoples of their native lands. The answer is probably a combination of the two.

In any case, each of these magical societies had their own wands and wandmakers. While the magical peoples of Asia (collectively known as the Nanwu) lived in highly isolated societies, their wands were clearly made by the same Wandmakers. Every wand from the Nanwu bears the same brand. For many years it was believed that one Wandmaker created all of the wands however documents show us that there was one settlement, high in the mountains of what is now Tibet, where all of the wands for the Nanwu were made.

The Sabril settlement consisted of hundreds of

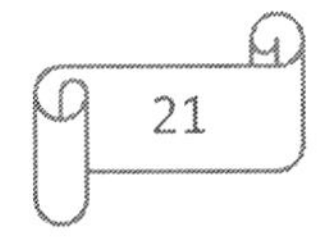

Wandmakers and it is their brand that appears on all of the Nanwu wands. (The Sabril settlement exists to this day, providing wands for the Asian continent as well as many of the wizard settlements of the Pacific Rim and the Pacific Islands).

Sabril wands were one-piece, narrow, and decorated with intricate designs. Due to the limited access to wood, Sabril wands were usually crafted from cypress which once grew in large quantities in the region. Cypress is, of course, the Wood of Life. The area was once covered by large cypress forests. Now, the only cypress forest that remains in the area is the Sabril forest (the Sabrils have magically disguised it as a vast, rock-strewn wasteland). Sabril wands are still often made from cypress but with the opening of trade, they are beginning to experiment with other woods. To this day, the best cypress wands come from the Sabril.

The Sabrils sold their wands throughout the region by travelling to the various wizard settlements. While it was a long held belief the Sabrils did this by travelling on foot it should be noted that the modern-day Sabrils are extremely adept at parkour. (This is the ability to appear or travel from place to place by magic. It is known as “apparition” in

England.) One would have to assume the Sabril used parkour to travel throughout the vast territory where their wands appear.

(Due to their extensive travels, the Sabrils also are known for their detailed histories of the Magical Societies of the East. Indeed, it is the Sabril library that holds the known history of these peoples.)

As mentioned above, the Sabrils eventually travelled throughout the Pacific Rim and the Islands. Histories show that these areas were not originally populated by magical peoples. It was the various settlements and societies on the Asian continent that explored and discovered these lands, establishing new settlements wherever they went. The lack of settlements can be blamed on the overpopulation on these islands of the dreaded Firanga and Iskanga (Fire and Water Dragons). Much of the southern Pacific Ocean and many of the Pacific Islands were overrun by these creatures, rendering the area uninhabitable. As the creatures were contained, the lands were settled and the legendary Sabril wands found their way into these distant lands.

Two of the lands that began to trade with the Sabrils

were the continent of Australia and the subcontinent now known as India and Pakistan.

Australia had a small, native population of wizards. These wizards were direct descendents of a band of old world exiles who landed on the island continent and established a tight-knit society. It is interesting to note that the Astrals (wizards of the Australian continent) used wands very similar to those of the ancient wizards. Their wands were staves, often six feet long. Another fascinating feature is their staves had wrappings identical to those found on the wands of the Mellas in North America. While there is no documented link, it is assumed that the Astrals spent some time with the Mellas prior to departing over the Far Western sea. (The Mellas eventually became completely integrated into the Salien, joining with the wizards of the Salien. Mellas documents were then merged into the great library of Albalon, which only recently was re-opened. It should be interesting to see if we learn more about the potential Mellas-Astral link once the extensive history has been explored.) The Astrals were insular, never leaving their vast island home however they did willingly open trade with the Sabrils, importing fine cypress staves and exporting indigenous plants the Sabrils used for potions and recipes.

WANDLORE

The second area that traded with the Sabrils was the Indian subcontinent, the Middle East, and finally northern Africa. Records show the Sabrils themselves limited trade to the subcontinent. It is believed the Pardaloga (wizards of the subcontinent) traded with the Sabrils and then carried Sabril wands into the eastern lands when they migrated into these areas. (Wizards of the subcontinent, the Middle East, and northern Africa are all of Pardaloga descent.) In any case, the Pardaloga and the Sabrils were closely linked. This is evident in the wands they both used.

The Pardaloga were the only wizards who did not use wood in their older wands. This was thought to be due to the limited amount of wood on the hot plains where the Pardaloga first lived. The elder Pardaloga also had a strong belief in the sanctity of the natural elements, using only fallen fruit, leaves, and branches.

The Pardaloga also lived in close harmony with the Chotsir. Chotsir are short and goblin-like though they are not related to western goblins (Libertusa). Chotsir have long ears, pointed noses, and pointed feet. They are well-known throughout the world for their craftsmanship and the ability

to create perfect crystals. It was these crystals that were used as wands by the Pardaloga. The crystals themselves were embedded with the natural elements from the indigenous trees and shrubs.

As the trade opened for Wandmakers, Chotsir crystals and Pardaloga Wands found their way into western wands. The Salien often use Chotsir crystals in their wands.

The Pardaloga began to trade with the Sabrils, providing native plants, flowers, and trees as well as crystals to the Sabrils (which in turn made their way to the Astrals, around the Pacific Rim, and to the Pacific Islands). The Sabrils used these elements to craft fine wands for the Pardaloga, incorporating the crystals into cypress wands so it now common to see cypress handled wands carried by Pardaloga. The Pardaloga Wandmakers were influenced by their Sabril brethren. After trade opened with the Sabril, Pardaloga Wandmakers began to use native woods in their wands. Modern Pardaloga wands combine elements from the old and the new.

Two more areas that made significant contributions to Wandlore and early wand history are the African

continent and the Amazon River basin in South America. These areas are the home of two very important innovations (for westerners) in wand history. The first innovation is due to the natural abundance of wand woods in these areas. Many of the woods used in wands around the world today come from these areas. It is from Africa that we first see ebony used in wands. (Ebony is the Wood of Power.)

The Kibojara (wizards of Africa) lived in large communities within the tribal settlements of the humans. (It was in Africa that wizards and humans lived side-by-side for the longest time often in perfect harmony. To this day, many communities remain completely integrated though the humans are not aware of the true identity of their neighbors.) The Kibojara had an abundance of woods to make their wands. It was the Kibojara who perfected the art of combining different woods into one wand. Many Kibojara wands are created from five to ten different woods.

Kibojara Wandmakers were often the leaders of their settlements. In order to make wands, the Kibojara Wandmakers needed an extensive knowledge of their surroundings. This knowledge was well-used by the settlements as they battled numerous enemies (magical creatures – especially Firanga, manticores, and gultogars and warrior tribes of humans, giants, and fallen wizards).

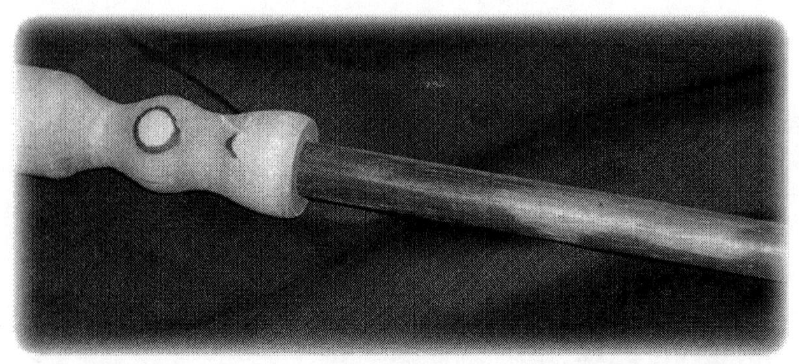

This is a Kibojara Wand. Note the different woods bonded together to create both the wand and the handle. This wand has pieces of ebony, mahogany, and yellowheart. The handle is a combination of yellowheart, and mahogany.

The Sabedora of the Amazon River basin were the first wizards to put elements from magical creatures into their wands. (Paddy O'Brien is largely given credit for this innovation by western wizards but the truth is the Sabedora were adding phoenix feathers, dragon whiskers, and more to their wands at least six thousand years before Paddy ever did.) The Sabedora were the guardians of the elements they lived around. Long before Europeans ever discovered the treasures of South America, the Sabedora were protecting

the rare creatures that lived side-by-side with them. It was in the Amazon basin that the first phoenixes were documented. (Phoenixes now prefer to live in arid, warm environments often situating their eyries on inaccessible cliffs.) A number of Firanga lived in the dense, warm forests of the Sabedora. The Sabedora also shared their home with pixies, mermaids, manticores, gryphons, basilisk, and salamanders to name a few.

Europe

European wandmaking was surprisingly unified and stable throughout the ages (in great contrast to the fractured human history of this area of the world). European wizards come from a single stock, the Galdorgalere. It is believed the Galdorgalere were descended from Salien wizards who did not join the Exodus plus Salien wizards who returned to the old country from Ocidenia Expona. In any case, within one hundred years of the Exodus, records show there was a small but thriving community of wizards based in the loch regions of modern-day Scotland. This clan grew and migrated to repopulate the lands of England, Ireland, and then onto the continent. By 5000 BCE, every country in

Europe had small settlements of wizards living among the humans. (It should be noted here that the wizards actually lived in their own communities. These communities were scattered among the human settlements. Of course humans of the era were much less sophisticated. The wizards hid their abilities from their human counterparts. But the wizard settlements were out in the open, not hidden as most present-day settlements are.)

As with all wizards, the Galdorgalere used wands. Galdorgalere wandmaking was historically concentrated in four major settlements – one in Ireland, one in Scotland, one in Austria, and one in Slovakia. (Note here I am using the modern names for these places. At the time, Ireland and Scotland existed as regions and entities, Austria and Slovakia did not. They were both part of the area generally known as the "Germanic Regions".) The Galdorgalere wands were what would be considered "classic wands". They were crafted from native woods. Galdorgalere wands had handles but no inserts, wrappings, or embellishments.

WANDLORE

This is a Galdorgalere Wand that was originally crafted circa 4250 BCE. This wand style is still very popular among the Galdorgalere today. The handle and the wand are hawthorn.

(Please note: We have only brushed the surface of the characteristics of each of the magical peoples and their wands. I have limited the discussion of the wizards to their contributions to Wandlore. For more information on the magical peoples, please see *Wizards and Magic, A Comprehensive History – Principles of Wizardry Volume Four*. For more information on magical creatures, please see *Magical Beasts, Monsters, and Creatures – Principles of Wizardry Volume Five*. For more information magical plants, please see *Magical Plants and Herbs of the World – Principles of Wizardry – Volume Three*. Finally, a comprehensive description of the Wands of the World and Wand Elements can be found later in this book.)

Each of these societies contributed to the development of the modern wand. However, it was the Salien who brought many of these elements from their original homelands into the accepted Wandmaking process.

The Great Journey

The Salien, as I noted, settled in Ocidenia Expona in 5580 BCE. For the next two thousand years, the Salien lived in peace and prosperity. Once they had established themselves in Ocidenia Expona, some Salien, led by the Wandering Elves, departed to explore the world. (The journey took place on elven-built ships – the finest the world has ever seen. It took over twenty years. The Salien departed in 5020 BCE and returned in 5000 BCE). During their extensive journey, the Salien made contact with every other race of wizards including the Sabril, the Pardaloga, the Astrals, the Sabedora, and the Kibojara. They collected plants and elements, crystals, and wood. They also studied the techniques of Wandmaking (as well as magic, weapons, and lifestyles) of the wizards they encountered. They documented the numerous creatures, plants, and societies.

(The Salien, brave warriors that they are, also fought in numerous battles aiding the wizarding realms they visited. Detailed accounts of this journey reside in the great library of Albalon. Perhaps one day, they will be organized into a book. The journey would make a great story!)

This journey was a key point in the development of the wizarding realms of the world. For the first time, the realms had contact with other realms. (Of course, at the time, there was no practical way to maintain the contact. Parkour only works over a limited distance. The Salien had not yet established their authority over time and time travel. It would be another 3000 years before large-scale travel between the wizarding peoples of the world would be possible.) The Salien returned with an in-depth knowledge of the art of Wandmaking from around the world.

For the next sixteen hundred years, Salien Wandmakers experimented with their newfound knowledge. They added crystals to their wands. They tried different woods, metals, and elements that their merchants gathered from the other societies. (After the Great Journey, the Salien established a brisk mercantile trade with their new allies. This trade, though limited, gave Wandmakers the first access to elements from non-local sources.) They combined elements and tried different techniques. Wands became much more diverse and Salien wizards were fortunate enough to be able to choose the style of wand they wanted. It should be noted that most Wandmakers of the time, while understanding the importance of wand elements, firmly believed the wizard choose the wand and the wand's power derived solely from the wizard. A Wandmaker's task was to find the perfect combination of elements for each wizard, to maximize the wizard's ability and power.

The journeys of the Salien also had an influence on the Wandmakers they met throughout the world. The Sabrils and Pardaloga in particular were fascinated by these visitors from so far away. It was at this point in their history that the Sabrils first began to explore the Indian subcontinent. From the time of the first visit of the Salien explorers, the Sabrils steadily widened the reach of their commerce and trade. This brought them in touch with the Pardaloga, who in turn began to expand their settlements to the east. As each of these wizarding peoples spread farther afield, they took their Wandmakers and wandmaking techniques with them.

WANDLORE

After the great Salien Journey, Galdorgalere wands went through a brief phase of various embellishments (though they did not use inserts from magical creatures at all until Paddy O'Brien's day). Wandmakers experimented with crystals and wrappings but returned to their classic roots within fifty years of the Great Journey.

But an important seed was planted. This seed would grow into fruition nearly six thousand years later with the establishment of the ISW.

The fates of the various wizarding societies rose and fell through the ensuing years. The Salien fought the War of the Three Powers. The Pardaloga became divided along tribal lines. All around the world, as the number of humans and human settlements increased rapidly, many wizarding realms found themselves on the run or forced into hiding. By 400 CE (Common Era), many areas of Europe, Asia, and northern Africa, as well as the Mediterranean, and some of the Pacific Rim lands had declared wizards to be "evil" or "the devil". Wizards found themselves hunted. Many of the realms hid their existence from their human neighbors. (They were so successful that most humans do not realize wizards not only exist, but thrive, to this very day.) A few wizards managed to live out in the open but many others retreated to wizard strongholds far away from the prying eyes (and often dangerous inclinations) of their human neighbors. Trade and travel between the Wizard Realms became difficult. This limited the exchange of knowledge. Wandmakers within each society continued to innovate and perfect their craft but separately, without the knowledge of their counterparts around the world.

The ISW and the Modern Era of Wandmaking

In 630 of the Common Era, Wandmakers joined together to form the International Society of Wandmakers. In a time when wizards were hunted throughout the world and wizarding society was split along national and cultural lines, the ISW became the first successful international group bringing together Wandmakers from throughout the world in common experience and mutual support. The ISW established guidelines for Wandmakers and Wandmaking, it disseminated information, provided capital and guidance,

and established a highly successful apprenticeship program. Even more importantly, the ISW protected the rights of Wandmakers and fought the trafficking of substandard wands. All wands sold to wizards should have the ISW certification.

The ISW was founded by three members of the Wandmaking community – VirgiFingal of the Salien, Tenzin Norbu of the Sabril, and Euan MacPhearson of the Galdorgalere. Each Wandmaker represented the finest in wandmaking skill and knowledge within their Wizard Realms. Meetings between the three were facilitated by the Salien ability to travel through time. (For more information on the Salien and time travel, please see *The Caledon Crystal* and its sequels.) The three met in the Sabril settlement at the request of Virgifingal. She realized the wizarding Realms of the world would be stronger if they united together to combat their common foe - ignorant, greedy, and selfish humans. As a Wandmaker, VirgiFingal (This apparently was not her true name, simply a moniker she adopted to protect her real identity which is known only to a few within the Salien Realm.) believed the common bond of wandmaking would bring together the varied wizards of the world. The three Wandmakers established the ISW to meet these ends.

The first meeting of the ISW took place in the great wizard school in Scotland, Pecgwyrt. (The Salien opened a special portal allowing Wandmakers from all over the world to attend.) After several days of feasting and sharing their knowledge (a first-hand report says the feasting took up most of the time), the Wandmakers representing every Wizard Realm around the world (wholeheartedly) joined the ISW. The ISW soon became the standard for wizard cooperation. Committees were formed and the ISW by-laws and standards were passed. (And then the feasting started again – or so I have heard.)

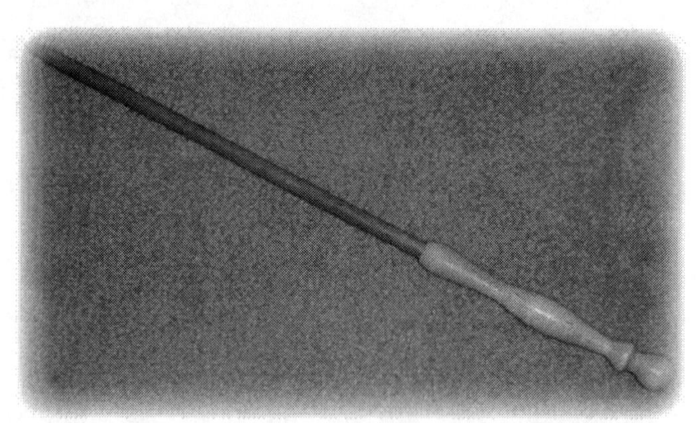

This is a Galdorgalere wand crafted in 627 CE by Euan MacPherson. The wand and handle are wych elm with a unicorn tail hair insert.

WANDLORE

In addition to the standards and by-laws governing Wandmaking, the ISW was also instrumental in opening up trade throughout the world. At first, the ISW was limited in their success since there was no accepted rate of exchange of the various wizarding currencies. Now, with the establishment of the League of Wizards (LW) and the Assembly of Unification of the Wizarding Realms (AUWR), Wandmakers have the ability to barter and trade for their woods and wand elements. (In 1796, after many decades of debate, the great Wizard Hamilton of the United States came up with a formula establishing a common exchange system for the various currencies used in the Wizarding Realms.) This has opened up the market for wand woods, crystals, and other elements. Wandmakers are no longer limited to those woods and elements commonly found within their home countries. The rise in availability has made even the most exotic woods common in Wand Shops around the world. In addition, the actions of the LW have made it possible for the best Wandmakers to sell their wands all around the world.

CHAPTER TWO
The Creation of a Fine Wand

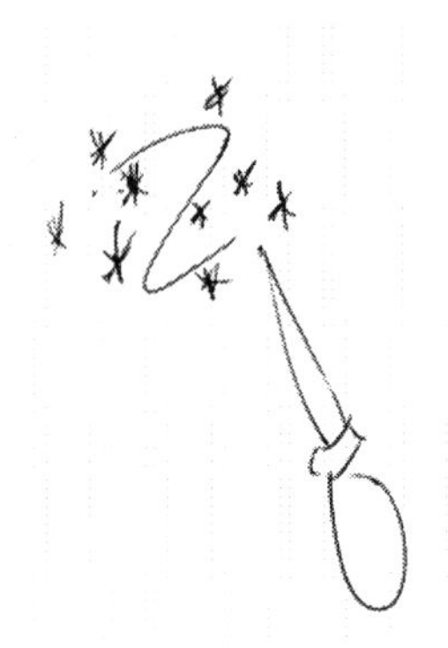

For most wizards, their first encounter with their wand is at a Wand Shop. But the life story of the wand begins well before this encounter. It starts with the Wandmaker.

A Wandmaker, by the strictest of definitions, is a wizard who creates wands. A true Wandmaker is so much more than this. The Wandmaker must study all of the world's woods. He must understand the uses for the woods, the combinations, and magical characteristics of the wood. She must learn the art of crafting the wood into the wand. A fine wand is a true work of art, perfectly balanced, carved to enhance the power of the wood, and tuned to fit its wizard.

For each wand, the Wandmaker chooses the precise piece of wood for the wand. This is done by instinct and experience. The piece of wood is then prepared for use in the wand. Some pieces are destined to become the handle and others to become the shaft. Each piece is important as the combination of woods in the handle and the shaft is the basis for the completed wand. (For those wands that have both handles and shafts.)

After the pieces are prepared (generally this means cutting them down to size and turning them into rounds), the woods are allowed to cure. Cured wood is more stable, a characteristic important to a wand. After the curing, the wood is ready for use.

We should take a moment here to discuss how a Wandmaker cures a wand. Curing is best accomplished using a levitation charm. The Wandmaker will suspend the pieces of wood in a curing cabinet and then employ a breezemaking charm to keep a continuous flow of air around the wood pieces. The woods are kept at consistent, precise temperatures specific to each type of wood. The curing process should enhance the power of each piece of wood. Every Wandmaker has their own secret curing formula and none were willing to share their secrets for this book (myself included).

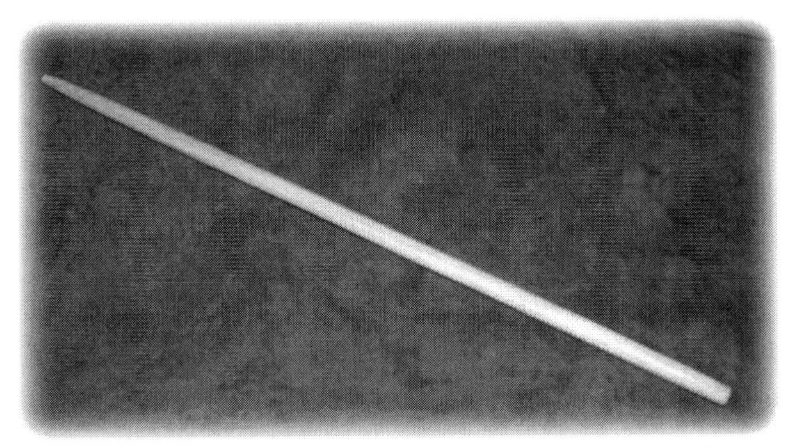

This is a cured wood wand. Note how it has already been shaped into the wand. It will now be mated with a handle and a crystal in the Salien Evadama style.

Once the wood has been cured, The Wandmaker will choose the individual pieces of cured wood for the wand and shape them into the wand and the handle. This is where the Wandmaker's artistry and craftsmanship are most imperative. The handle design must enhance the powers of the wood. The wand itself must have a perfect balance in the hands of its wizard. The weight and the length of the wood must be combined in the correct way to achieve this perfection. An unbalanced wand will feel awkward to the wizard. This in turn will affect the wizard's ability to use the wand.

I cannot stress the importance of the design and execution for the functionality of the wand. The true Wandmaker handcrafts every wand individually, no wand is mass produced. Anyone (even non-magical humans) with enough skill can carve or turn a piece of wood and make it *look* like a wand, only a true Wandmaker can create a true wand.

The process of crafting the wand is another secret Wandmakers are reluctant to share. The spells used by each Wandmaker are considered some of the greatest secrets of the trade. Wandmakers will often use vague terms to throw the curious off of the scent. (I, personally, tell everyone I hand-turn my wands using a lathe. This is a human machine for turning and shaping wood. It is an excellent cover for my real techniques.)

Every Wandmaker has their individual style. The wizard should be able to tell who made their wand just by looking at it for the Wandmaker's characteristic features (I would say character) in the design. The Wandmaker learns their craftsmanship through study and apprenticeship, the Wandmaker learns their art through experience.

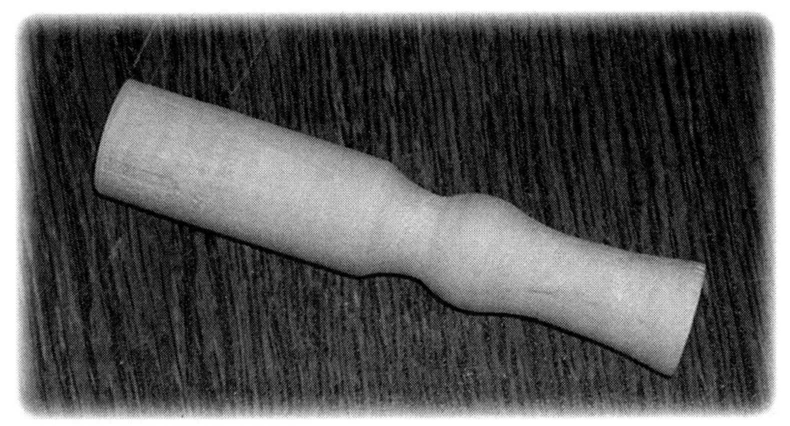

This is a basic wand handle crafted from Rowan. The handle has been cured. It will be mated with a wand. Since this is a Galdorgalere wand, an insert will be added. The wand will then be cured and finished.

Once the individual pieces of the wand have been crafted, the Wandmaker bonds them together. In some

instances, cores from magical creatures are inserted prior to the bonding. Other cultures prefer crystals or other enhancements for their wands but the purest wand is one made from wood and only wood. (Wand elements and their uses will be discussed in Chapter Seven of this book).

The wand is then set aside to cure again. After curing, the Wandmaker will finish the wand. Finishing may involve wrappings. Some wands (those of the Sabril) have intricate designs on them. But (this is very important), true wands are NEVER stained or painted in any way. (I bring this up specifically for any humans who may be reading this book. The human market has seen a recent influx of low quality, human-made wands. These mass-produced wands are made from cheap, low grade woods and then painted. These con artists paint the wood and call it ebony, or willow, or bloodwood, et cetera. This is not important to wizards as they would never purchase a wand from a non-ISW certified Wandmaker but humans are taken in by this practice. Even worse are these so-called wands made of some human material known as "resin". Don't even ask me what I think of these toys! A note to all the humans reading this book, if you want a true wand, even though it will not perform magic spells for you, get one from an ISW-certified Wandmaker.)

WANDLORE

Once complete, the Wandmaker will test each wand for functionality, feel, balance, and of course power. The wand then waits for that special day when its wizard claims it.

Wandmaking is a labor-intensive process. It takes time. Obviously, this is reflected in the price of the wand. However every wizard knows a fine wand is worth the price.

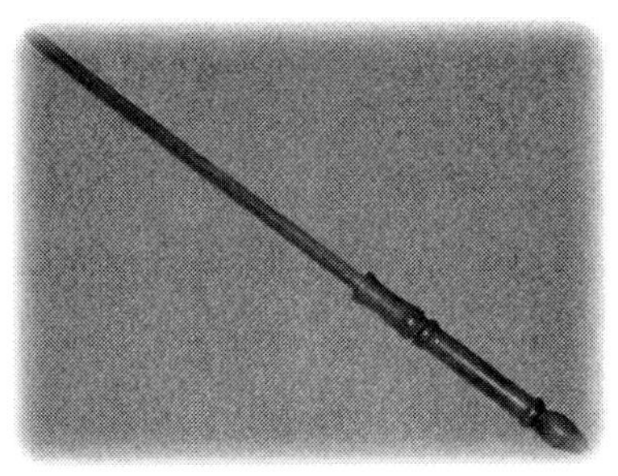

This is a finished wand, ready to meet its wizard.

PRINCIPLES OF WIZARDRY
VOLUME ONE

CHAPTER THREE
The Wand-Wizard Bond

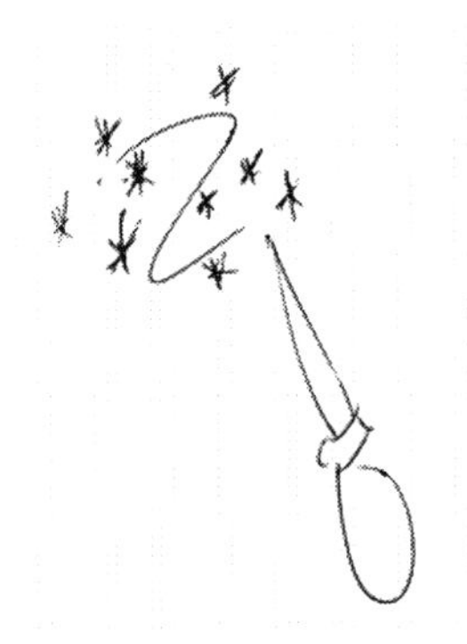

Wizard-Wand ownership is a long-term (often life-long) relationship. The bond between wand and wizard is only broken when the wand is destroyed or damaged beyond repair or when the wand is removed from the hands of its wizard or when the wizard dies. The bond between wand and wizard has been studied for centuries and it is still an area where we have large knowledge gaps. We do know there is a special bond between the wand and its wizard. (Wandlore is based on the study of the wand. Therefore the relationship is considered here from the wand's point of view.) We have studied how that bond grows over time until the bond comes to full power as the wand and the wizard operate in complete unison.

Theories of the Wand-Wizard Bond

For hundreds of years there were two major competing theories on the wand-wizard bond - the Killarney Theory and the Petrov Theory.

The Killarney Theory was first hypothesized by the great Wandmaker William Patrick "Paddy" O'Brien from Killarney, Ireland. Born to large wizarding family in 1632 CE, Paddy O'Brien spent his earliest years in a small cottage on the shores of the Atlantic Ocean. Paddy showed signs of his future genius by crafting his first wand at the age of three. After that first wand, he made wands for his twelve brothers and sisters, his extensive family, and his friends. Soon his parents were receiving requests for "Paddy Wands" from wizards far and wide.

When Paddy was six, he and his family moved to the

town of Killarney to join the large (undercover) wizarding community based there. It was in Killarney that Paddy gained fame for his exquisitely crafted wands. Wizards travelled from all over the world to purchase an authentic Killarney wand.

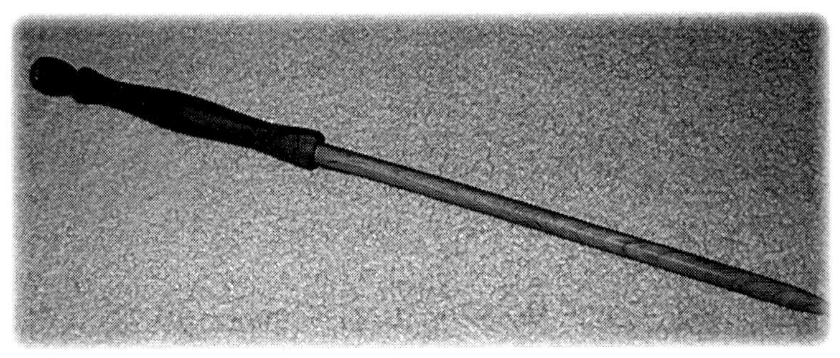

This is a Paddy O'Brien Killarney Wand. The wand is cedar and the handle is walnut. The insert is unicorn tail hair. Paddy made this wand in 1667. He was experimenting with insert and wood combinations at the time. Note the flowing design of the wand. This is in direct contrast to Petrov's wands which tended to be angular with strong lines.

Paddy himself travelled extensively, collecting woods for his wands. When Paddy was in his late teens, he travelled to Africa to the famous Phoenix Colony. There he befriended Romulus, his lifelong companion. On the return journey, Paddy was hit by a sudden idea.

"It was as if a massive stunning spell hit me," he later reported. "I was struck dumb with the idea of putting one of Romulus' feathers into my Hawthorn wand."

As soon as he got back to his Killarney workshop, Paddy went to work. Two days later, Paddy had created the very first (western) wand with a magical core. His wand quickly became famous throughout the Galdorgalere Realm for its power and durability. Paddy believed the combined powers inherent in the wood and the magical cores enhanced each other when they were properly mated. Paddy continued to explore and refine his theories for the remainder of his long life.

In his continual studies, Paddy became convinced the wand had a personality or a magical spirit of its own. This concept was controversial in its time as Galdorgalere wizards thought only wizards had magical spirits (magical souls). This widely held belief relegated other magical beings such as elves, goblins, leprechauns, fairies, and all others to a lesser, soulless level of magic. Paddy believed differently. His close friendship with Romulus allowed him to observe the magical abilities and potential of non-wizards. Romulus,

like all phoenixes, had prodigious powers of his own. Paddy believed some of these powers melded with the power inherent in the wood of his wands. These combined powers gave the wand its own magical spirit.

As a magical entity all its own, Paddy formulated the theory that it was the wand that chooses the wizard. The Killarney Theory hypothesizes the magical spirit of the wand lies dormant until their one, true wizard picks it up. At this point, the wand's magical spirit bonds with the wizard's magical spirit. This was evident to Paddy as the magical sparks of excitement that would fly from a wand when it met its true wizard. (Of course we have all seen this phenomenon.)

There are limitations to the theory. As all wizards know, they can pick up any wand and make it work, though the power and accuracy of the spells may be affected if it is not "their" wand. But the wand will still work. Paddy's explanation was the magical soul of the wand, if forced, would work no matter who the wizard wielding it was. But the wand itself would stubbornly refuse to work properly for any but its true owner.

Paddy was so convinced of a wand's soul and ability to act on its own and with its own agenda, he would refuse to have a discussion with anyone who doubted his theory. In fact, Paddy never considered the Killarney Theory a theory at all. When, late in life, he wrote his lengthy memoirs, the ten chapters in which he lays out his theory are simply titled "*The Magical Soul of the Wand - the Complete Truth*".

Paddy O'Brien was considered by many to be the greatest Wandmaker who ever practiced the art and science of Wandmaking. Paddy never married and he never had children, leaving as his legacy the thousands of Killarney wands spread around the world. Most of these Killarney wands have been lost; it is likely they were interred with their owners at death, as Paddy's own wand was. This was the last piece of Paddy's theory. He believed the magical soul of the wand, the spirit of the wand, was broken by the death of its owner, thereby rendering it useless.

WANDLORE

This wand is a famous Killarney Wand. While it is in the Paddy O'Brien style, many believe it was actually made by Nikolai Petrov while he was Paddy's apprentice. The wand and handle are both of elder, the insert is phoenix feather. This wand is one of the few wands that have been passed from wizard to wizard (contrary to the Killarney Theory). This wand has a bloody history and is coveted for its rumored power. Once again, it has disappeared but it is sure to surface again. It is sometimes called the Wand of Destiny.

Paddy's other legacy were the dozens of Wandmakers around the world he trained during his life. Most of his apprentices did not live up to Paddy's reputation. Paddy was unapologetic, stating, "You can teach a wizard to make a wand, but if it is not part of his spirit, you can't cast a spell to give it to them. You either have it or you don't."

One of Paddy's apprentices certainly "had it". Nikolai Petrov would be Paddy's greatest triumph and also his greatest heartbreak.

Petrov, like Paddy, came from a large wizarding family in what would be modern day Poland, born in 1872 to a Russian father and an Irish mother. Young Nikolai, by all accounts, was precocious, often casting spells on unsuspecting humans (completely against wizarding laws, of course). His mother explained away his youthful indiscretions, "It wasn't like he was harming the humans in any way. He just got them to give him extra sweets and things like that." Still, Molly knew her son was one step away from spending considerable time in reform school so she packed him off at the age of ten to her relatives in Ireland. (Nikolai was the youngest of Molly's twelve children until shortly after Nikolai was sent away, when Molly proceeded to have triplets. Nikolai believed his mother no longer loved him and simply sent him away to make room for his younger siblings. He was so distraught when he heard of the birth of his brothers and sister; he never spoke to his mother again.)

Away from the indulgent attitude of his doting

mother, Nikolai appeared to thrive. A gregarious and outgoing child, he soon settled into the life of his new, loving (but very strict) family. Ever fearful of being sent away again, he cast about for a necessary skill, one he could depend on to make a living, even though he was still very young. He attended the local wizard school where he excelled at spells and care of magical creatures. It was in this class at the age of thirteen that Nikolai came to the notice of Paddy O'Brien.

Paddy was making a grand tour of Ireland, promoting his theories on the magical soul of non-wizard beings. One day while Paddy was giving his lecture, he became annoyed with young Nikolai, who appeared to be fidgeting and not paying attention. Paddy confronted the young man, only to realize he was repairing a classmate's wand that had found itself on the wrong side of a backfiring curse. Paddy was so impressed with the skill shown by young Nikolai he immediately offered him the position of apprentice in his Killarney shop. Nikolai gladly accepted the opportunity (with the support of his foster family). He moved to Killarney and studied with Paddy for the next five years.

While Paddy refused to discuss his former

apprentice, friends of Paddy's remember the two of them as inseparable.

"They were like father and son," remembered Tad Mullaney, a neighbor of Paddy's. "Two peas in a pod. Paddy was delighted to find a young man with so much potential and Nik was happy to have a warm bed and an attentive father figure in his life."

Following ISW guidelines, Paddy trained Nik in all aspects of Wandmaking, reportedly even sharing secrets he had never shared with any others. As time wore on, Paddy let Nik do more and more of the actual Wandmaking while he travelled and lectured on the art and science of wands - especially on the magical soul of the wand.

"Maybe that is what finally did it," Tad Mullaney says. "Nik wasn't the type of guy who would let anyone take credit for his work. He was grateful to Paddy for giving him direction and a chance but I don't think he liked working to promote someone else's fame."

Friends of Nikolai claim he was completely loyal to Paddy but a strain was developing in their partnership.

WANDLORE

"It was never a partnership," Evgeni Duprov, a close friend of Nikolai's claims. "That was the problem. The old guy had Nik working his fingers to the bone while he took all of the credit. I wouldn't have stayed. Nik did the right thing."

"Hogwash," Jane Pendleton, housekeeper for Paddy O'Brien says. "Paddy was great to that boy. Nikolai made his fortune while he was working with Paddy. Any young wizard would have leapt at the chance to inherit Paddy's estate. Nikolai was too impatient, too greedy. Luckily Paddy saw it before it was too late."

Whatever the cause, Paddy O'Brien and Nikolai Petrov would part ways in early 1703. Paddy would live another one hundred and two years. In all of that time, he never once mentioned Nikolai's name. When he died, Paddy left his considerable fortune to several wizarding schools to establish Wandmaking classes and research programs in his name. He left the rest of his estate to the Phoenix Colony of South Africa.

After leaving Killarney, Nikolai travelled extensively. So strong was his hatred of his former mentor, Nikolai was

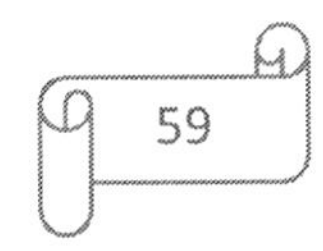

determined that his name, Petrov, would eclipse that of Paddy O'Brien's in the wizarding world. After years of travel, when his actions were largely undocumented (Nikolai himself only said he was doing "research into his theories" during that time.), Nikolai finally settled in eastern Russia, near the modern city of St. Petersburg, where he established his own Wandmaking Workshop and School.

Nikolai eschewed the theories of Paddy O'Brien in many ways. He felt there was little mystery to the art of Wandmaking. "It is a technical job," he wrote in his memoirs. "The actual act of making a wand is purely technical. The difficult part is bringing the wand to life, imbuing it with magic."

Nikolai believed the wand had no soul, no magic of its own. (To give Nikolai his due, he did believe non-human magical creatures had magical souls. His detractors widely spread the rumor he believed otherwise but this was simply not true.) Nikolai believed, and his theory states, that a wand is a completely inert object. It is the touch of its wizard that brings it to life, releasing its magical abilities.

"It is the responsibility of the Wandmaker to craft

the perfect wand for his customer," Nikolai writes. "If sparks do not come out of the wand at first touch, the Wandmaker has failed in his task."

The Petrov theory continues, "A wand has no free will and it certainly does not have 'feelings'. The wand is a tool, a weapon, in the hands of the wizard. If a more powerful wizard forcibly takes, either by magic or by hand, the wand, the wand will then bend to the will of its new master."

The Petrov theory says the wizard chooses the wand. In this school of thought, the wand is simply an inert piece of wood, waiting to be brought to life by the wizard. This theory says the wand is merely the fulfillment of the wizard's dreams or desires. Petrov stated the first wizard to touch the wand imbued the wand with some of his or her powers, thus giving it a magical identity. Petrov's theory also states that the first wizard who touched the wand, and each subsequent wizard, transferred some of their powers into the wand. The wand was like a sponge, absorbing these powers. This is what gave the wand the appearance of having powers of its own.

In Petrov's theory, the first wizard to touch the wand would of course be the Wandmaker. Therefore, every wand the Wandmaker creates is imbibed with a bit of the Wandmaker's own powers. It is this power that the wizard then "feels" when the wand is picked up. Petrov believed this power was retained even after the Wandmaker released the wand. Petrov's theory does not allow for any innate powers from the wand itself.

Clearly Petrov was refuting the teachings of his former mentor. So forceful was he on the concept of “no magical soul was possible in inanimate objects” and creatures that he became tagged as a Togib. This was patently untrue but the slander, once said, stuck to Petrov. Countries with large populations of non-wizard species banned him, including his former home of Ireland. Nikolai Petrov was so troubled by the slander and his treatment that he eventually closed up his shop and disappeared from public sight. He died at the early age of eighty-four years, by all accounts a spiritually broken man.

WANDLORE

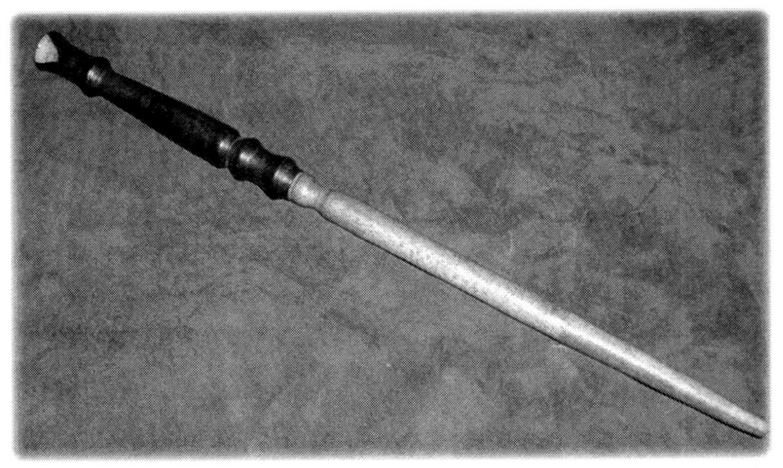

This wand was crafted by Nikolai Petrov in 1707. The wand is elder and the handle is ebony imported from the Kibojara. Note the strong lines and the detail work at the wand-handle junction. The insert is dragon heartstring.

For nearly one hundred years, the two stated theories, Killarney and Petrov, competed for dominance in the wandmaking world. Many wizard settlements had at least two Wand Shops, one in the Killarney tradition and one in the Petrov tradition. Wizards were forced to choose which they preferred. The ISW, not willing to referee the fray, did not have an official position on the competing theories.

Finally, in 1897, ninety-two years after the death of Paddy O'Brien, a young wizard from the United States, by the name of Wilson Abraham decided to study the competing aspects of the two theories. After more than ten years of study he concluded that BOTH of the theories were correct, in part. Abraham's studies showed Paddy O'Brien was correct in that wands do have magical souls. This is true as long as the wand is made from wood. (Chotsir crystals were examined by Abraham in later studies. The crystals also exhibited evidence of magical spirits but not to the extent of wood wands. Once natural elements were added to the wands, especially wood handles in conjunction with the crystals as most modern Pardaloga wands are, the wands had a magical soul equivalent to wood-based wands. The ISW has commissioned new studies into the magical properties of wood and elements, especially the Chotsir crystals. Once the studies are complete, they will be included in future editions of this book.)

Abraham's Law takes into account that trees themselves have spirits. While most of the spirits of the trees in the human world have long been dormant, spirits of the trees are quite active in wizard-protected forests such as the great Cypress Forest of the Sabrils and the many wand wood forests protected by wizards around the world. When Abraham travelled to the Cypress Forest, he was shocked to find the wood nymphs were willing to come out and communicate with him (nymph language is different from all other languages but the Sabrils are fluent in it). Abraham realized all trees had nymphs (even those in human hands), most were simply driven into hiding due to the human influx and the human devastation of the forests. (After concluding his studies on wand theory, Abraham spent the remainder of his life seeking out the nymphs of the forests of the world. He was writing a book on the subject when he met an untimely death at the hands of a mountain troll. The manuscript and detailed map of his nymph studies is currently located at the great Salien library at the Fort of Tigart.)

Once Abraham proved the spirits of the trees still existed, it was a small leap to show the spirits of the trees lived on in the wood the trees donated for wand use. (Every true ISW certified Wandmaker takes an oath to only use donated wood from giving trees.) Abraham tested his theory once again in the cypress forest of the Sabril. There the nymphs confirmed the presence of the spirit of the tree within the wands.

Supporters of Paddy O'Brien rejoiced when word leaked out of this discovery. However, Abraham also believed that Petrov was correct and he set out to prove that the wizard had great influence over the magic, and the magical soul, of the wand.

Abraham based his studies on scientific experimentation. He gathered one hundred basic wands (no inserts, no wraps, and no crystals - just plain wood). He first let humans (non-wizards) try the wands. Much as he expected, there was no "magic". The humans could not perform even the most basic spells (provided by Abraham) with the wands.

Abraham then gave the wands to four control groups of twenty-five. Each group was instructed to use the wands as their "regular", everyday wand. The first control group used the wands for one day, the second for one week, the third for one month, and the fourth for a whole year. (The wands were not matched to the wizards in any way and most wizards reported the wand felt awkward to use, not at all like their own wands.)

Abraham brought in a second test group of one hundred wizards. He divided the wands among this second group of wizards, instructing them to use the wands daily. The wands that had been in the hands of their control group for the least amount of time were the first to work properly for their "new" owners. The wands that had been in the control group for a whole year caused the most problems for their new owners. The wizards reported overwhelmingly that the wands would not perform spells or the spells were imperfect or they rebounded on them. (Needless to say, Abraham instructed the wizards to be cautious.) Some of the comments from the wizards who got the long-use wands included, "The wand felt as if it was fighting me" and "It felt like it was someone else's arm at the end of my own" or "It just wouldn't work. It didn't feel right."

Abraham concluded from this first experiment that the wands had "learned" who their wizard was and would not work for their new owners. The time frame for the greatest amount of wizard-wand bond was between the one month and one year groups, though the one day and one week groups did report a "breaking in" period of, on average, three weeks. Twenty-one members of the year-long previous owner test group never felt the wands were truly theirs.

Abraham was curious to see if the wands would "remember" their rightful owner. After allowing the second test group to use the wands for six months, he returned them to the original control groups. The long-term (one year use) group had the most success in wand control. In fact, twenty-one of the original owners reported their wands worked perfectly right away. The four who did not were the same four wands who seemed to have changed their allegiance to their second owners. The wizards who had only used the wands for a day (in the original control group) reported these wands did not feel like their wands, though the wands seemed to vaguely “remember” these previous (albeit brief) owners. Most wands would cast spells but not very accurately.

From these experiments, Abraham concluded the wand itself had a magical spirit, just as Paddy O'Brien believed. The wand also absorbed powers from its wizard, like Petrov said. But the real question was: Did the wand have a soul before it was mated with its wizard?

WANDLORE

Abraham conducted this experiment using wands crafted from four different Wandmakers from four different magical societies (Salien, Galdorgalere, Pardologa, and Sabril). Each of these Wandmakers crafted five wands. Each of the five wands was identical, crafted from single sources that were treated identically during the wandmaking process. Once the wands were completed, the Wandmaker conducted a series of tests and carefully recorded the responses of the wands. The Wandmakers concluded that each wand reacted the same way. The Wandmaker then "released" all of the wands.

Every Wandmaker kept one wand as a control. Abraham distributed the other wands to the other Wandmakers. Each Wandmaker was then asked to adapt the wand using their specific crafting techniques. For example, the Salien wand had its crystal removed by the Galdorgalere Wandmaker and a phoenix feather was inserted. The Sabril bonded scenes into the wands they received. The Pardologa added Chotsir crystals, and the Salien put in Elegia crystals. Each of these wands was "released" by the second Wandmaker and then returned to the original Wandmaker.

Abraham theorized that the wands would react differently after having been altered as compared to the control wand held by the Wandmaker who crafted it. He was correct. The Wandmakers conducted the same series of tests on the wands. Every Wandmaker reported that every wand worked differently in every way. Every wand was different, not only from the control but also from each other. Furthermore, the four changed wands were different from how they acted when they were first tested. The Wandmakers themselves reported the wands had changed in a deep, magical way.

From these tests, Abraham concluded the wand did indeed have a magical soul of its own and the soul was directly related to the Wandmaker who made it as well as to the elements and the wood the wand was made from. In other words, the wand had an innate spirit that bonded with and absorbed powers from the spirit of its wizard.

Even without scientific testing, Wandmakers believed the truth was somewhere between the two extremes of the Killarney Theory and the Petrov Theory. (Although there are still Wandmakers, most notably those in England, Scotland, and Ireland, who adhere to the Killarney

Theory and Wandmakers in Romania, Albania, and Russia who adhere to the Petrov Theory.)

Like all long-term relationships, the wand-wizard bond is one of mutual attraction. The wizard often has an idea of what they want in a wand - powers, appearance, favorite woods and elements. The experienced Wandmaker uses this knowledge to choose the wands the wizard will try out. The Wandmaker also uses their knowledge to help the wizard narrow down potential wand choices. At this point, the wand and the wizard choose each other. The mutual bond is formed by a mutual desire. This creates the most powerful wand-wizard bond. The wand comes alive when its wizard first touches it. For a Wandmaker, this moment is purely sublime.

One final aspect of the Wand-Wizard Bond we must mention is the “won” wand. This is a murky area of Wandlore but one we are aware of. There are times and circumstances where a wand that is “won” – forcibly removed from its wizard by another wizard using either magic or (rarely) physical force – will immediately change allegiance to the new wizard. This change of allegiance, if it occurs, is complete. In other circumstances, the wand will remain loyal to its original wizard. The new wizard may be able to work spells with the wand but they will lack power.

The reasons behind this phenomenon are unclear. Petrov believed it was a matter of the relative power of the wizards involved. This has been disproven numerous times throughout history. Caerth Malus, for instance, "won" Glindril's wand in their battle. However it was widely reported the wand was useless to Caerth Malus, so much so that Caerth Malus discarded it with Glindril's body. Wand and body were recovered intact by the Verdadama. (The wand was buried with Glindril.) It can be argued that Glindril was, in fact, the more powerful of the two wizards (even though he was killed in the battle). There is no way of knowing this but I tend to think that relative power was not a factor (especially in this case). I think Glindril's wand refused to be won over by Caerth Malus. It knew its wizard and it would not change allegiance.

Other wands have a documented history of being won over by new wizards. (The Galdorgalere Wand of Destiny is one of the most famous wands in this category.) Some Wandmakers believe it is inherent in the wand itself if it can be won over. Perhaps the characteristic is enhanced or activated by the Wand-Wizard bond? The ISW continues to study this phenomenon but I will not be publishing the results of the study (should there ever be any). This information would be too powerful to dark wizards and others who may want to use it for their own gain.

Wand allegiance is an imprecise area of wand ownership widely studied by Wandmakers (without conclusive results). Most wizards know the first “owner” of the wand is the Wandmaker who crafted it. As Abraham proved in his experiments, it is possible for a wand to change its allegiance (though the wands were sometimes reluctant to do so). The length of time the wand is in the hands of the wizard apparently is a factor.

The crafting of a wand is a deeply personal experience for the Wand and the Wandmaker. The wand will naturally be bound to the Wandmaker who created it, yet wands purchased from Wandmakers almost always change their allegiance to their wizard. The ability of the wand to do this was a mystery to wizards (but not to Wandmakers) for many ages.

There have been several documented cases of wands

refusing to relinquish their allegiance to their Wandmaker. The most notable, of course, was the great Wandmaker, Calumzel the Third in 265 of the Fifth Age (Salien) who inadvertently created havoc when 10,129 wands he crafted for the Army of the Green Mountains refused to work, leading General Lekian to near defeat (hand-to-hand combat and a small core of wizards with non-Calumzel wands provided cover allowing almost all of the Army to withdraw).

At the time there was no definitive explanation (to the general wizarding public) as to why a wand will refuse its new wizard. For the first time ever, I can reveal how Wandmakers force their wands to change their allegiance to their new owners. The Wandmaker must "let the wand go", and willingly give up the allegiance to the wand, thereby "releasing" it for its wizard. This is imperative, as seen in the Calumzel case. Calumzel was so proud of his craftsmanship, he loved his wands so much, they were unable to change their loyalty.

Early in my own career, I performed an experiment (that Abraham would have admired). I crafted twenty wands, ten of which I "released", the other ten I did not. All ten released wands performed as expected. The unreleased wands would not work at all for the wizards.

One of my testing subjects reported, "It never felt like the wand was mine."

The Wandmaker must release the wand for it to accept its wizard. (In theory, a wizard could release a wand but this has never been tried and there really would be no reason to do it.) The act of "releasing" the wand is a deeply personal, secretive, and protected moment between Wand and Wandmaker. I cannot say more.

CHAPTER FOUR
The Care of Your Wand

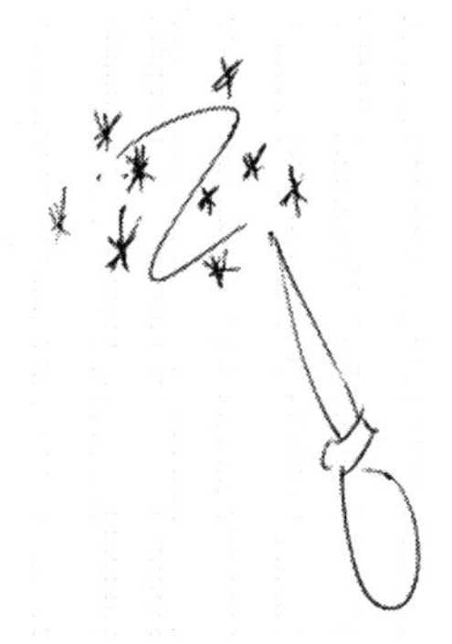

Wand care is a very touchy area for Wandmakers as we are well aware that most wizards do not properly care for their wands. Yet a properly cared for wand will reward its wizard with superior performance.

Wand care is actually not very difficult. The ISW recommends using a wand care kit for regular maintenance. The kit should contain a Wand Oil and a soft application cloth. All wands should be polished at least once a week using a single drop of oil. Gently massage the oil into your wand. (Please note: If your wand does not have a shiny finish, this will not make it shine.)

Storage of your wand is another issue. Most wizards just toss their wand down next to them when they go to sleep. This is not recommended. First, you should always keep your wand in a place that is easily accessible should you need it during the night. Second, this place should be in a wand bed. Wand beds are made from a soft material. The material is nestled in a box (without a lid for easy access). Your wand should be properly put to bed every night. It should also be gently wiped down to remove any debris from your (apparently too-busy-to-properly-care-for-your-wand-
-the-very-wand-that–may-save-your-life-one-day) busy day.

If, for any reason, you will not be using your wand for a length of time (though unimaginable, this would, in theory, be possible), please store it in its wand bed with the lid on. I would also recommend a locking charm and maybe even a secret spoken spell to keep your wand safe and sound until you use it again.

At least twice a year, your wand should be inspected

by a Wandmaker (preferably the Wandmaker who created your wand). The Wandmaker will perform a thorough examination of your wand, identify and correct any problems or injuries, and tune it up. Most wizards completely skip the wand examination but it really is imperative for optimum wand performance.

Treat your wand properly and take care of it. Your life may depend on it.

CHAPTER FIVE
Wandmaker Training and Certification

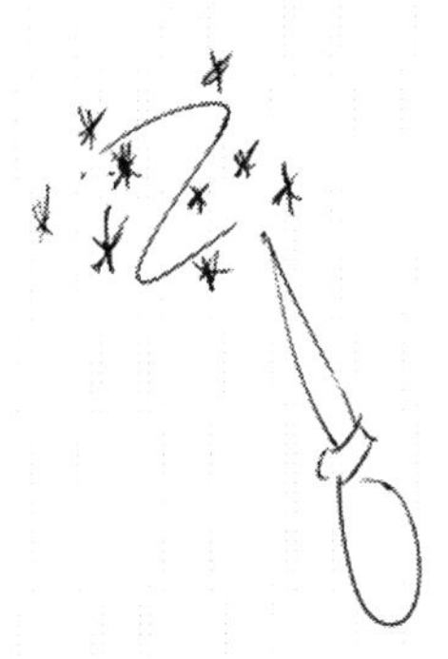

The ISW has established policies for Wandmakers and the training of Wandmakers. Throughout the ages, Wandmakers have apprenticed with experienced Wandmakers to learn their craft. The ISW has institutionalized this policy with great success.

Training as a Wandmaker is a lifetime endeavor, usually starting from the earliest of ages. It is often said that Wandmakers are born and not made and this is largely true.

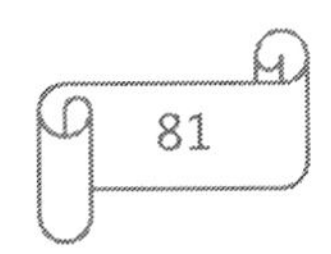

Every Wandmaker working today showed skill and interest at a very early age, usually by the age of three or four (true years ... As all of you are aware, the lifespan of a wizard is considerably longer than the lifespan of a human.) Young wizards who are identified as potential Wandmakers are tested by the ISW. If they pass the “natural talent” test, they are assigned an apprenticeship with a Master Wandmaker (this usually occurs no earlier than the age of eight and most commonly at eleven years old). They will live, work, and travel with the Master Wandmaker for the remainder of their training (in close connection with their families who often move with their budding Wandmaker). Apprentice Wandmakers, known as Parnha, study the art, craft, science, history, and practice of wands and wandmaking. Once they are deemed ready by their Master (with a minimum training period of twelve years unless special dispensation has been given), they take the final test. If they pass, the ISW then promotes them to Senior status.

The new Senior Wandmaker is then required to travel the world, visiting Master Wandmakers in the various wizarding societies to observe their techniques. The Seniors learn how to handle magical creatures and collect elements and wood. (Many Senior Wandmakers from the West,

myself included in my time, enjoyed the time spent with the Chotsir the most. Their work is fascinating.) It is important to note that the Senior Wandmakers are not necessarily made privy to the spells used in the wandmaking process. This trip is meant to add to their knowledge of wandmaking. They will work with the Wandmakers around the world but often as Parnha.

This trip normally takes two to three years. When the Senior Wandmaker returns to their Master, they usually spend three to six months with their Master as they prepare to go off on their own (this is also an excellent opportunity for the Master to find out about new wandmaking techniques and innovations). Once the Master deems them ready, the Senior petitions the ISW for an available position. The ISW convenes three times a year for a super-secret, special ceremony where Senior Wandmakers are promoted to Masters. (The ceremony is based on ancient Salien and Sabril traditions. It involves the sharing of secrets known only to Master Wandmakers. It also involves much eating and drinking.)

Every Wandmaker since the founding of the ISW has been trained in this method. The only (small) exception to

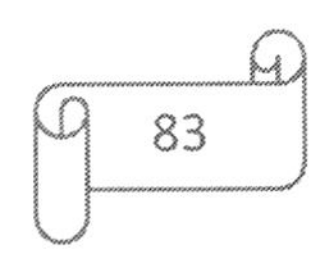

the accepted ISW training guidelines are the Sabrils. Sabrillian Parnha all move to the Sabril compound in the Himalayas to train with their Master at the age of eight. The Sabrils have been training Parnha this way since 7680 BCE with great success.

The newly ordained Master Wandmakers often get to choose the location of their Wand Shop. However, the ISW must approve the location. This is not, as has been surmised by humans, an attempt to protect the older Wandmaker's business. As wizarding realms spread out or contract, the need for Wandmakers does as well. The ISW strives to assure the availability of a Master Wandmaker for every wizard settlement around the world.

Master Wandmakers also have the option of moving their Wand Shops to new locations. Once again, the ISW is petitioned for permission which is almost always granted. (A notable exception to this was Nikolai Petrov's petition to set up a competing shop in Killarney after his world tour. Petrov had not informed the ISW of his location during his years of absence and was therefore on probation. Of course the ISW would never allow a second Wandmaker in Killarney as the community was being well-served by Paddy O'Brien.)

CHAPTER SIX

Wands Around the World

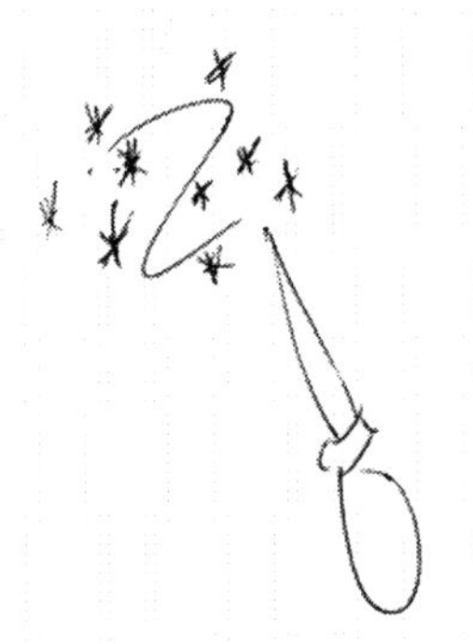

We will begin our journey with one of the two oldest Wandmaking sites in the world.

Sabril Wands

Sabril wands were carved from a single piece of wood. The most common wood in Sabril wands is Cypress. Thousands of years ago, an extensive cypress forest covered this area of the Himalayas. Much of this forest, like so many others, was destroyed by the influx of humans. The Sabrils

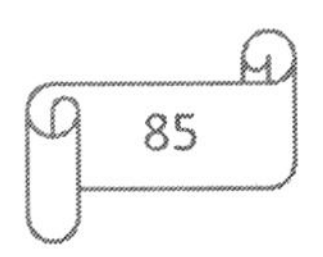

hid a large section of the forest from the human invaders and protected it. Cypress is the Wood of Life and the Sabrils firmly believe their very existence depends on protecting their cypress forest at all costs. As trade was opened, the Sabrils incorporated other woods into their wands but every Sabril wand, to this day, as some cypress in it.

Sabril wands are a continuous taper from thick to thin. One interesting feature of the Sabril wands are they are not completely round. All Sabril wands are squared off, with four flat sides that taper to round approximately halfway down the wand. Sabril wands always end in a fine point. Sabril Wands are extremely narrow and delicate but strong. (The strength of the wand here means unbreakable. One should remember that wizards have ways of strengthening wood and wands that human science cannot explain.) Sabril wands are always ten to twelve inches long.

Since the Sabrils were limited in their wood choices for so long (thousands of years), they devised other methods of incorporating the powers of various elements into their wands. Sabril wands are “decorated” with a technique that bonds colorful pigments (the Sabrils will not divulge the source of the pigments) into the wood itself. The

Sabrils are true artists with this technique. Each wand depicts four themes, one on each side of the wand – plant, animal, elemental, and historical. The Sabrils harmonize the scenes to bring out the optimum power in each wand. The elements depicted on the wands enhance specific powers in the wand.

In developing and perfecting this technique, the Sabrils overcame several disadvantages they faced with their wandmaking. They were largely isolated within their mountain compound with limited access to outside resources. Their finely detailed artwork brought the same enhancements into their wands that wrapping or inserts did for the wands of the Mellas and the Galdorgalere. It is important to stress that the designs are not merely painted on the wands (in the human fashion). They are bond into the wands using spells known only to the Sabrils. In fact, these spells are so well protected that only the oldest and most respected of the Sabrils can perform them. Many a Wandmaker has tried to replicate the Sabril wand without success.

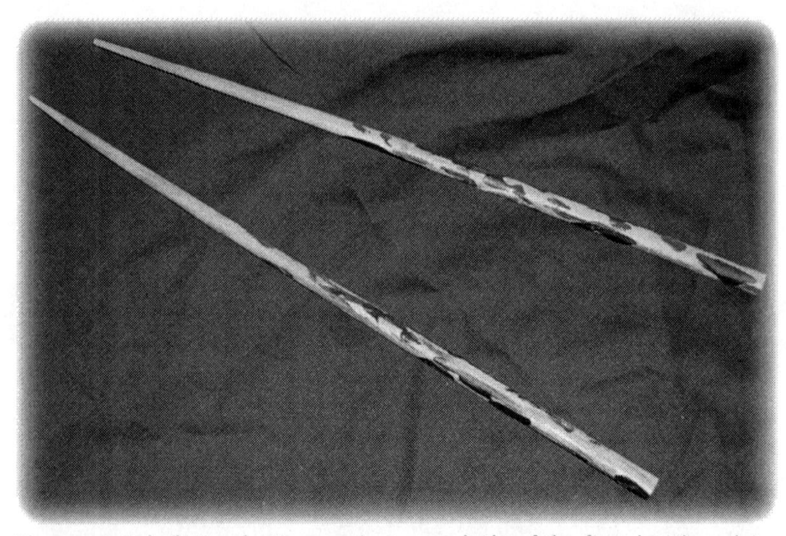

These are Sabril Wands. You can just see a little of the fine detail work in these wands. The wand at the forefront features a depiction of the Battle of Qalak. The wand in the rear has flowers of the Golden Champah.

The wizards who use the Sabril wands (called the Nanwu) usually have two wands – general use and fighting. Though the Nanwu lived in peace for thousands of years, they eventually were forced to protect themselves from humans and various creatures who infringed on their lands. The Nanwu aided the Sabrils in the conquest of the Taping Islands and the defeat of the Huolonguajia. They used specialized wands for these battles, made by the Sabrils.

WANDLORE

Sabril wands are truly unique in the wizarding world. As trade has opened up, Sabril wands, more than any other specific wand, have become a showpiece for wand collectors worldwide. (Even humans collect these wands. In fact, there are quite a few humans who collect wands from around the world, a phenomenon created by an interest in the wizarding world that exploded after the publication of a controversial expose of details of the existence of wizards. This has caused numerous problems for the various Wizard Realms. It has also been the root cause in the rapid rise of fake wandmakers. On the other hand, sales to humans are an easy source of income for Wandmakers.) Sabril wands are light with a bouncy feel, a factor that throws off many western wizards.

The Galdorgalere

The Galdorgalere also have a long, documented history. Thought to be descendents of the wizards who did not leave in the Exodus (and therefore related distantly to the Salien of North America), the Galdorgalere have lived in established settlements for many thousands of years. The

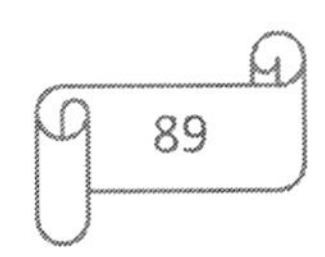

original Galdorgalere wand was a basic wand with a basic handle. Throughout the years, Galdorgalere Wandmakers have incorporated different techniques and ideas from around the world into their wands.

Modern Galdorgalere wands have many styles and looks. They are always made from wood. The Galdorgalere have access to many species of deciduous and conifer trees throughout their lands. The Galdorgalere always make their wands from a single wood, they do not mix woods or have a different wood for the wand and the handle. (Though the wand and handle are most commonly created separately and then bonded together. This technique allows for a stronger wand as wands created from a single piece of wood that is carved into a wand and the handle tend to be weak at the wand-handle joint. Wandmakers have long tried to correct this problem using various spells without much success.) Some Galdorgalere wands are handleless. Galdorgalere wands may have wrappings though this is by no means a common feature.

WANDLORE

This is a modern Galdorgalere wand, crafted from holly with a holly handle. Note the natural finish and shape of the wand handle. This is one of the many styles of Galdorgalere wands that are popular today.

The single feature common to all Galdorgalere wands is the insert. Every Galdorgalere wand has an insert from a magical creature. The most common inserts are from dragons, unicorns, and less frequently from phoenixes and Vilas. The reasons for this are simple. There are large populations of dragons and especially unicorns in Europe. The major Wandmakers of Europe have long traded in the magical elements they put into their wands. As you might imagine, it is not easy to collect some of these elements. (I, for one, always use a dragon wrangler when I collect my dragon whiskers, scales, and barbs.) Vilas, of course, are the

one magical creature used for inserts in Europe who can speak. A Vila must willingly give her hair to be used in a wand, a rare event. The second rarest of the inserts are phoenix feathers. There are only about fifty phoenixes in all of Europe right now. Phoenix must give their allegiance to a specific wizard and this does not happen very often. The phoenix also must willingly donate a feather for wandmaking. This is an uncommon occurrence. As such, Wandmakers often divide the phoenix feathers they have for use in more than one wand. (Few Wandmakers are willing to admit this practice.)

Galdorgalere Wandmakers commonly use unicorn tail hair and dragon heartstring in their wands. (The Galdorgalere are the only wizards who use the heartstring of the dragon for wands. The rest of the world deems this to be too barbaric. Other Wandmakers use dragon whiskers, dragon wing scales, and dragon tail barbs with great success. Tail barbs in particular are gaining in popularity, even among the Galdorgalere.) Dragon elements add strength to a wand (and in the hands of a dark wizard, dragon elements add ferocity to the wand). Unicorn tail hairs, in contrast to a hair from another part of the unicorn, add an element of accuracy to the wand. Less common (simply due to the

limited supply) are phoenix feathers. Less than fifteen percent of all Galdorgalere wands have a phoenix feather insert though the phoenix feather is a very strong component to any wand, increasing the intensity of the spells worked with it.

Galdorgalere wands are usually ten inches to about sixteen inches long. Every wand has a different feel but most would describe Galdorgalere wands as stiff but springy. The wand handles range in size from three to six inches. Galdorgalere wands have a wide range of looks and finishes (though they are never stained or painted), some are completely natural and others are highly polished. As with most Wandmakers, Galdorgalere Wandmakers are now using woods from far-off lands. While they still prefer the woods that have served them well for ages, some Galdorgalere wands are now available in such exotic woods as ebony, rosewood, teak, and acacia, to name a few.

The Astrals

As I mentioned earlier, the Astrals were an insular

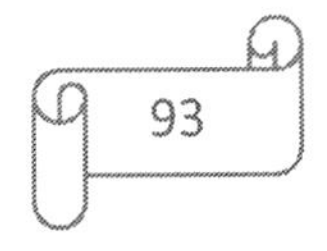

society based on the island continent of modern-day Australia. The Astrals carry staves and use them as wands. The Astrals lived in rugged, untouched territory and the staves served numerous purposes. They were used as wands, of course. But they could also be used as physical weapons (you don't want to get knocked on the head with a stave) and as a means of support while travelling over the tough terrain of the Astral homelands.

Astral staves are created from the native woods of the lands. The most popular woods in modern Astral staves are eucalyptus, oak (known for its durability and weight), cedar, and ash. A stave must be properly fit to its wizard. The perfect length for a stave is the height of the wizard plus or minus one head length.

WANDLORE

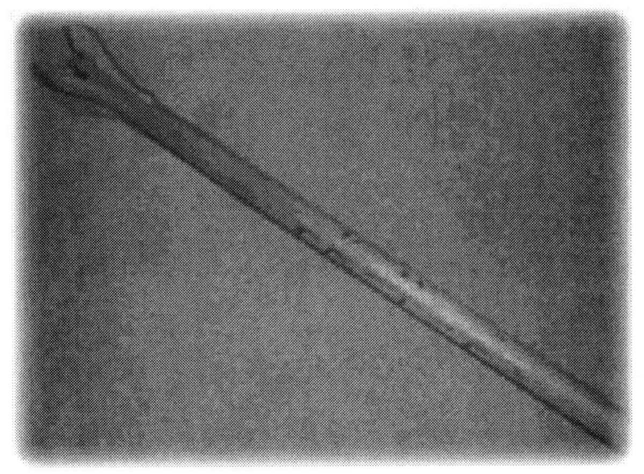

This is a modern Astral stave. The total length of the stave is six feet six inches long. You can see some of the bonded wrappings from the crimson waratah on the stave in the very center of the picture. This stave also has a Chotsir crystal nestled in the top.

Astrals get their first stave at the relatively young age (for wizards) of five years old. This first stave is often created from eucalyptus, which has strong protective elements. The first stave is one head shorter than the wizard. At the age of eight (the average age worldwide when most wizards get their first wand), the Astrals get their second stave. Once again, the second stave is almost always made from eucalyptus. They keep this stave until the age of eleven when they receive their third stave. This stave may be made from eucalyptus or ash. Finally, at the official coming of age for the wizard (seventeen), the wizard meets their adult or permanent stave. This adult stave is full-size.

Traditional Astral staves are kept in their natural state though they are finely finished (using a sanding charm). The staves are round, with a flat bottom. The bottoms are often coated with metal (to prevent wear). The Astrals always wrap their staves with natural elements. The wrappings are most commonly plants though some Astrals use metals for their wrappings. Favored wrappings of modern Astrals are leaves from oak and beech trees, needles from pine trees and leaves, flowers, and vines from the scarlet firewheel, the golden-red banksias, and the crimson waratah.

Like the wrappings of the Mellas, the elements are bonded with the stave. Since the opening of trade, the Astrals have begun adding crystals to the tops of their staves in the Salien or Pardaloga tradition. Some Astral staves are now highly formed, with latticework, shapes, and crystals topping the staves though the wrapping has remained in the traditional manner.

The Pardaloga

The Pardaloga also have a long, well-documented history. Elder Pardaloga wands were made completely from crystals with natural elements (mostly plants, vines, and especially flowers) embedded into the crystals themselves. The Chotsir make exquisite crystals. (Their craftsmanship is so fine that Chotsir crystals appear in virtually all wizarding societies today. In addition to making wand crystals, the Chotsir make almost every crystal ball used by wizards around the world.)

Elder Pardaloga wands were comprised completely of embedded crystals. The crystals were long and rather thick. They were opaque near the handle and transparent through the wand. The embedded elements were easily seen throughout the wand. (It should be noted the embedded elements were placed individually within the crystal wands. The designs are very intricate and quite beautiful.) The most popular elements of the oldest Chotsir wands were vibrant flowers from the shrubs and plants that dotted the hot landscape. Red silk cotton flowers, trumpet flowers, leaves and flowers of the Shivalingam, and

Moonbeam flowers were the most popular choices but the Chotsir would use any plant or leaf available to them.

The next generation of Chotsir wands used magical creature elements almost exclusively. (Like all wizarding peoples, there are trends in wandmaking – wand "fads" as it were - with various elements, designs, woods, and concepts gaining and then losing favor. Most modern wands incorporate the best of these trends though Wandmakers are always on the lookout for ways to improve their wands.) The most popular choices were fur from the Sidhe and feathers from the Firgara and the hamsa.

Eventually, Chotsir Wandmakers integrated both plant and creature elements into their crystal wands. In any case, these elements performed the same function as different woods, inserts, and crystals do – they enhanced the power of the wand in very specific ways. The Pardaloga would choose their wands in the same way that wizards do all over the world. From the very beginning, the Pardaloga believed in the magical soul of the wand. (This was largely due to their close relationship with the Chotsir who, in other wizarding societies, would have been treated as less significant than wizards. At certain points in wizarding history, the Chotsir would have been segregated and relegated to those magical creatures without a true magical soul by some wizarding societies. The Pardaloga never believed this and always treated the Chotsir as equals.) The Pardaloga firmly believed the wand chose the wizard (and still do to this day).

The Chotsir will not discuss any of the methods they use to create their crystals. It is well-known that Chotsir magic is different from wizard magic. Numerous Wandmakers have tried to replicate the Chotsir crystals without success. (It is important to note that while the Chotsir created wands for the Pardaloga for years, the Chotsir do not believe they are Wandmakers, they are Crystalmakers and remain so to this day. The ISW has extended membership to the Chotsir but the Chotsir still prefer to be known as Crystalmakers. The Chotsir do not carry or use wands.)

This is a photograph of Chotsir crystals used in wands other than the Pardaloga wands. Note the exquisite craftsmanship. Chotsir crystals are often faceted.

Chotsir crystal wands were not long by modern standards, ranging in size from seven to ten inches. Chotsir wands were unbreakable by normal means (as are their crystals and their crystal balls). However, Chotsir crystals can be melted and destroyed by a direct hit of fire from a dragon or by cursed fire.

The Pardaloga continued to use the elder Chotsir wands until the Sabrils arrived. The Sabrils were unsuccessful in establishing a thriving trade with the Pardaloga in wands. (The Pardaloga preferred their Chotsir crystal wands to the Sabril wands.) However the two wizarding peoples did found a trade in raw materials and supplies. (The Chotsir began trading in crystals and crystal balls with the Sabrils, spreading their fame along with the fame of the Sabril wands.)

Pardaloga Wandmakers were fascinated by the Sabril wands and began incorporating wood into their own wands. At first, the wood was embedded in the crystals. Eventually, Pardaloga Wandmakers began to use the wood as handles with the Chotsir crystals as the wands. The crystals continued to have elements embedded in them (and they still do to this day). With the advent of the handled wand, Pardaloga Wandmakers came into their own. Working in close cooperation with the Chotsir crystalmakers, Pardaloga Wandmakers created truly beautiful and functional wands.

Pardaloga wands are, on average, ten to fourteen inches long. The handles are always four or five inches long. The crystal wands, which are six to ten inches long, are opaque near the handle and transparent at the tip. The crystals are embedded with natural elements, most commonly a mixture of plant and creature elements. The crystals are faceted, never round. (Chotsir crystal wands were always faceted.)

One of the most popular elements of Pardaloga wands is the Vanjhvala (Flame of the Forest). This tree produces bright, flame colored flowers which the Chotsir add to the crystals. Magical creature elements the Pardaloga use are the dragon, mermaid, and salamander scales, feathers from the firgara, hamsa, and muninn, and hair from pixies. The most popular creature element used by the Pardaloga is the fur from the sidhe. Woods used by the Pardaloga are teak, palm, asoka, and nim.

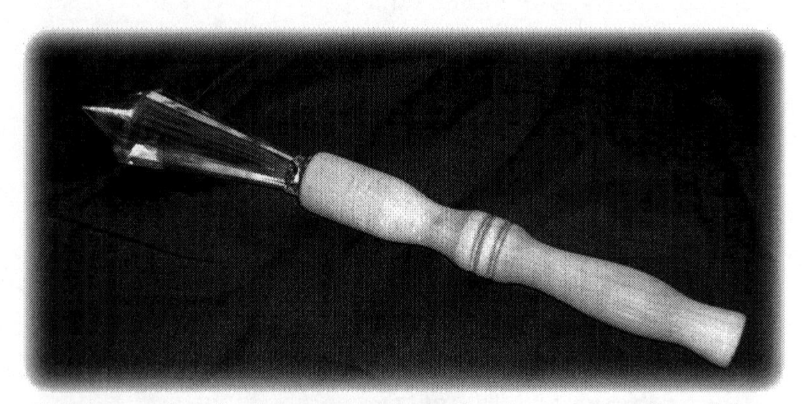

This is a modern Pardaloga wand. Note the nim wood handle and the Chotsir faceted crystal with flowers from the Flame of the Forest and fur from the sidhe.

Pardaloga wands are truly unique in the wizarding

world. The harmonious use of plant, wood, creature, and crystal has been unmatched by any Wandmakers in documented history.

The Kibojara

The Kibojara are the wizarding peoples of Africa. The Kibojara originally lived in the sub-Saharan regions of the continent, now known as central Africa, and the southern lands of the continent down to the southernmost tip. The Kibojara lived in harmony with the humans that settled around them. The Kibojara were held in high respect by the humans, most likely due to their extensive knowledge and fighting abilities.

The Kibojara lands were (and are) home to numerous species of wood, plants, and magical creatures. (The Kibojara, like all wizarding peoples, officially went into hiding approximately 1300 – 1400 years ago. Many Kibojara still live among the humans but they keep most of their abilities hidden like the rest of us.) The Kibojara share their homelands with exotic species of wood such as ebony, tulipwood, bloodwood, pink ivory, yellowheart and more. (I

am using the common, human names for these woods.) Plant life is extensive in the region. In addition, Kibojara Wandmakers have direct access to numerous magical creatures.

Kibojara Wandmakers used every element available to them. Kibojara wands are most remarkable for their seamless integration of numerous woods into each wand. Kibojara wands regularly have five to ten different woods. Some of these wands are crafted from a single species of wood but the individual pieces are donated from different trees. Other Kibojara wands are made from up to five different species of wood. The Kibojara Wandmakers use secret spells to bond these woods together to make a solid whole.

WANDLORE

This is a Kibojara wand with handle. The handle has three different woods bonded into it (ebony, redheart, and yellowheart). The wand is crafted from mangrove and laurel. All of the woods have the essence of dragon scales.

Every piece of wood is gathered and cured in much the same way as woods used by Wandmakers the world over are cured. The Kibojara Wandmakers then carve individual pieces of wood and fit them together like a puzzle. The pieces are then bonded with each other and the wand is allowed to cure again. Once the second curing is complete, the wand is finished and ready for its wizard. Kibojara wands are extremely hard, with a firm feel. Kibojara wands are twelve to twenty inches long, with smaller wands available for underage wizards. Kibojara wands are thicker than most wands, they average about three-eighths to one half inch in diameter. Early Kibojara wands did not have handles but after the Great Journey, handles began appearing on Kibojara Wands. Modern Kibojara use wands both with and without handles.

Another key component of the Kibojara wands is the use of other elements during the curing process. Kibojara Wandmakers will add plant and creature elements to their curing cabinets. The magical properties of these elements are absorbed by the wood during the curing. Once again, the Kibojara Wandmakers were unwilling to have their methods printed here. I was fortunate enough to be made privy to this procedure by four Kibojara Wandmakers. I can tell you the claims are true. The woods do absorb the magical characteristics of the elements during the curing process. I have been sworn to secrecy on the process itself but the Kibojara have permitted me to use the process myself, as long as the secret dies with me, although I am currently negotiating to allow one or two apprentices to be trained in the Kibojara methods. (An additional aside to all of the Wandmakers out there who have been trying to replicate this process, you are not even close!)

This absorption process is used to maximize the

power of the individual pieces of woods that are then used in the wands. The most popular elements used in Kibojara wands are phoenix feathers and dragon scales. This is, of course, due to the large protected populations of phoenixes and dragons on the African continent. The Kibojara are the protectors of the single largest colony of phoenixes and the second largest colony of dragons. (The colony in Romania is still the largest but the Kibojara colony will probably surpass it within the next fifty years.) The Kibojara also use Firgara feathers and muninn feathers, and salamander scales. Common plants elements used in the curing process are Moonbeam, palm leaves, and flowers and leaves of the Ixora and the Skyflower. Each of these elements is carefully matched to the corresponding piece of wood. The woods are then bonded together to make the perfect wand.

Kibojara wands, like all other wands, can now be found worldwide.

The Sabedora

The Sabedora first resided in the Amazon River basin in what is modern-day Brazil. (They have since migrated north and south and now extend throughout modern South and Central America straight up into Mexico.) The homelands of the Sabedora were rich in magical plants, creatures, and wood, all of which the Sabedora Wandmakers used in their wands.

Sabedora wands are similar to the wands of the Galdorgalere yet they appear to have developed their wands independently of one another. Sabedora wands are six to twelve inches long with very short, round handles. The wands are heavy with a crisp feel.

The Sabedora were the first to use inserts in their wands. Historical records indicate they first used inserts in 6234 BCE. This innovation is accredited to Tuia Wanadi, the famous Sabedora Wandmaker. Tuia lived in the Sabedora settlement of Merma Dalis. She grew up, as most wandmakers do, crafting wands by hand for her family and then her neighbors and friends. At the age of twelve, she was appointed the Wandmaker for Merma Dalis. (This was prior to the establishment of the ISW and its training program.) Even though Tuia was young, she continued to experiment with the quality and character of her wands.

WANDLORE

When Tuia was fifteen her father, Pacan, had an encounter with a Gryphon. (The Sabedora are guardians of all of the creatures within their realm, magical or not. They do not believe in harming a creature unless they have no other choice. This is known as the Edict of the Sabedora and most wizarding societies adopted it with the founding of the AUWR.) Following the Edict of the Sabedora, Pacan fought the Gryphon until it was tamed. As a token of his friendship, Pacan gave the Gryphon (from this point on known as Apaec) a collar crafted from his own hair. In return, Apaec gave Pacan a headdress crafted from fur from his tail. (Apaec became the first Gryphon in South America that could speak. This was a gift from the Sabedora. Even though Gryphons are sometimes speaking creatures, the Sabedora still use fur from Gryphons in their wands. The Gryphons, of course, donate the elements to the Sabedora Wandmakers.) Tuia decided to use a piece of tail fur in her father's wand thus beginning the Sabedora practice of using inserts in their wands.

From this point on, every Wanadi wand had an insert. Tuia used the scales of the salamander, hair from the xanas, and feathers from the Hamsa and Phoenix. Of course, Tuia continued to use the fur of the gryphon. Modern

Pardaloga also use unicorn tail hairs. This is a direct influence from the Galdorgalere.

Once Tuia had found the proper pairing of magical creatures and woods, she began to add magical plants and flowers. By combining elements, Tuia found that negative properties of certain creatures or plants could be counteracted by their counterpart in the pairing bringing out the best in each element. Tuia also found that the pairing were very specific in size and quantity. She also discovered only certain pairs worked.

This is the first wand with an insert created by Tuia Wanadi in 6234 BCE. Note the short round handle. This wand is crafted from pink ivory with an ebony handle. The insert is Gryphon tail fur given to Tuia's father by Apaec, the great Gryphon King.

While many of these pairings are Wandmaker secrets, the Element Tables in this book give you some guidance to complementary and antagonistic elements.

The Mellas

Mellas history is not well documented in the general magical history. This is due to the fact that all ancient Mellas documents are housed in the great library of Albalon. This wondrous city has been hidden for thousands of years as the Salien fought Caerth Malus. What we do know of Mellas history has been handed down in the oral tradition from the Mellas to the Salien. This oral history is rich and detailed in many aspects but not in Wandmaking. After the great Salien Exodus, Mellas history was documented by the Salien.

The wands of the Mellas, like the rest of Mellas society, were absorbed by the Salien by 1899 BCE. From this point on the Mellas were completely integrated into the Salien. Many Salien traditions are undoubtedly rooted in Mellas history and traditions as was much of Mellas Wandlore. However, of all of the great wizarding peoples, only the Mellas have been completely absorbed by another society. Sadly, most Mellas wands from before the Exodus and through 1899 have been lost to time. (There are rumors that thirteen Mellas wands have been preserved in the vaults of Esgalon.) Reproductions of Mellas wands, made in the oral tradition, have been created, including the one pictured here.

What we do know about Mellas wands and Wandmakers is the extensive use of wrappings on their wands. The Mellas only used magical plants, usually pieces of Indian grass (the most common element used in Mellas staves), the leaves of the walking fern, the flowers and leaves of the lilium, the berries of the obavata, and the flowers of the goldthread and the calamint. The Mellas combined the elements to enhance the power of the wand. Some Mellas wands had elements embedded on the tip, creating a crowning effect.

Mellas wands were a cross between a wand and a stave. The wands were between eighteen inches and thirty-six inches in length. They were of a uniform width (approximately two to three inches in diameter.) The Mellas held their wands one fist length from the tip of the wand, not down in the handle area. This part of the wand was narrower and fit precisely to the hand of the wizard. The wood used for the wands was carefully rounded and spell-sanded to a natural finish.

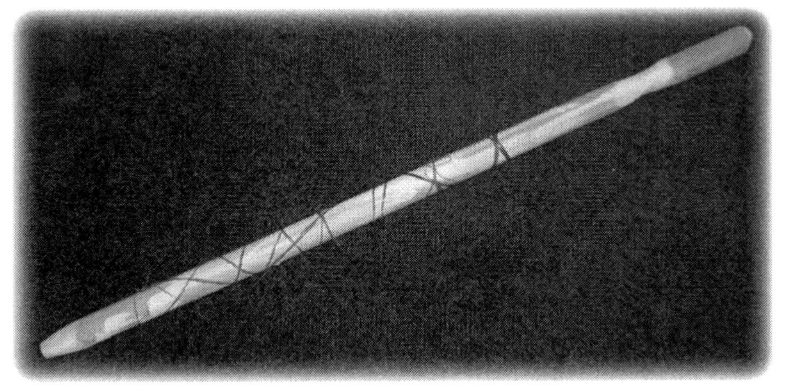

This is a reproduction of a Mellas stave. It is crafted from pine with Indian Grass wrapping. The stave is twenty-five inches long.

Perhaps, if they actually do exist, the wizarding world may one day see the Mellas wands held by the Salien.

The Salien

I have saved the Salien for last for several reasons. First, the Salien are the oldest documented living wizarding peoples, the oldest known Wandmakers were the elves who are among the Salien peoples of the current day, the Salien were travelers who brought back knowledge from Wandmakers around the world and employed them in their own wands consequently the Salien currently have the widest variety of wands of any known wizarding peoples, the Salien history is well documented, and finally, I personally have an extensive knowledge of Salien Wandmaking and Salien Wands. (Yes, I am a Salien. I am a Reyvensena in case anyone was wondering.)

WANDLORE

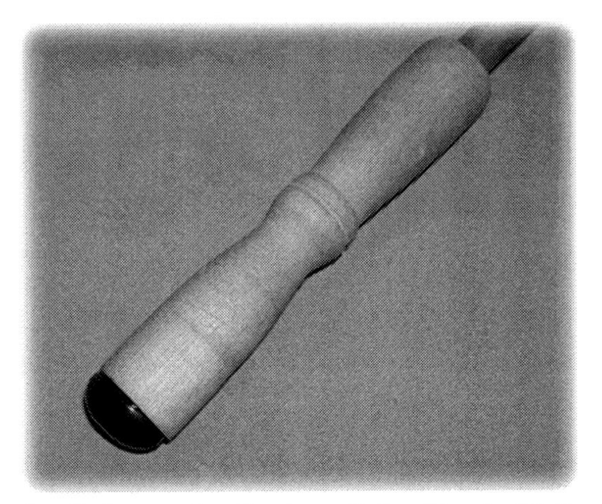

This is a detail picture of an Evadama Salien Wand with the crystal embedded at the end. The wand is cypress with an olive handle. The crystal is Elegian crafted from naryacrisa.

Salien wands prior to the Great Journey were uniform among all of the Salien peoples. The wands ranged in size from six to twenty-four inches. The smallest Salien (the Pauladama) carried wands that were six to eight inches long. The Pumilla's wands were ten to twelve inches long and much thicker. The Evadama and the Libertusa carried wands that were thirteen to twenty- four inches long (The longer wands were carried exclusively by the Libertusa.) The Salien of the time used wrappings on their wands. The wrappings were paired with the native woods that were plentiful in Ocidenia Expona. The wands had handles that were often decorated with jewels and crystals. As I mentioned before, modern Wandmakers consider these wands to be too busy. It took the Salien Wandmakers another nine hundred years to come to the same conclusion.

When the Salien returned from the Great Journey in 5000 BCE, they brought with them knowledge and wands and elements from all of the wizarding peoples they encountered. At first, the Salien Wandmakers attempted to incorporate the various techniques and elements into their wands. After two or three years of experimenting, they came to the conclusion that less was more. Luckily for the Salien Wandmakers, they had four distinct *loga* to make wands for. (There are seven Salien peoples or *loga*. At the time of the Great Journey, there were five loga. The Elegia do not use wands. The Eximia became Salien in 4288 BCE at the end of the fifty year war between the Salien – Mellas armies and those of the Cawr. The Verdadama became Salien in 2415 BCE at the time of Glindril's death. Glindril's story is another tale that needs to be told.)

The Pumilla (dwarves) soon favored Kibojara-style wands. Pumilla wands are stout and thick, about eight to ten

inches long and an inch and a half in diameter. They do not have handles and the wands are a continuous taper from the handle to the tip. The tips are one-half inch in diameter with a flat end. They are crafted from six to ten different pieces of fused wood but they also have a single magical creature element. The most popular elements among the Pumillas today are dragon, gryphon, and hippogriff. The wands are always precisely ten inches long.

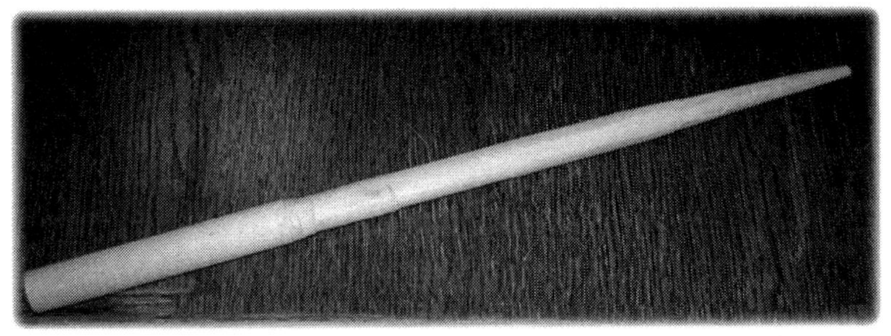

This is a Salien Pumilla wand crafted from a single piece of oak, ash, and maple. The element is hippogriff feather. Note the thick wand with the long taper. The handle area is only slightly thicker than the wand itself and is part of the wand, not a separate entity.

The Libertusa (goblins) use Sabril-style wands. Their wands are thin, no more than three-eighths of an inch at the base, and they taper to a point. The wands are made from single pieces of wood. They are either squared or round at

the bottom end and taper to round. Every Libertusa wand has the word for freedom bonded to it (Libera). The wands range in size from fifteen to twenty-two inches. There are no handles or inserts in Libertusa wands, the wands are pure wood. (While many Elegia and Evadama Wandmakers cater to the Libertusa there are still four Libertusa Wandmakers making wands for the Libertusa today.)

This is a modern Libertusa wand crafted from redheart. This wand was made by Kreieren, a Libertusa Wandmaker.

The Pauladama carry handled wands with a distinct and separate wood for the handle and the wand. The two woods are perfectly matched and work in harmony. The wands are small by wizard standards, six to eight inches, but they fit the stature of the Pauladama perfectly. Pauladama wands also contain a magical element inserted between the wand and the handle. The most common inserts in Pauladama wands are hairs from pixies or fairies. Pauladama wands are narrow, the handles are a little larger than one half inch in diameter and the wands are just under one-half inch in diameter. The wand tapers to a rounded point.

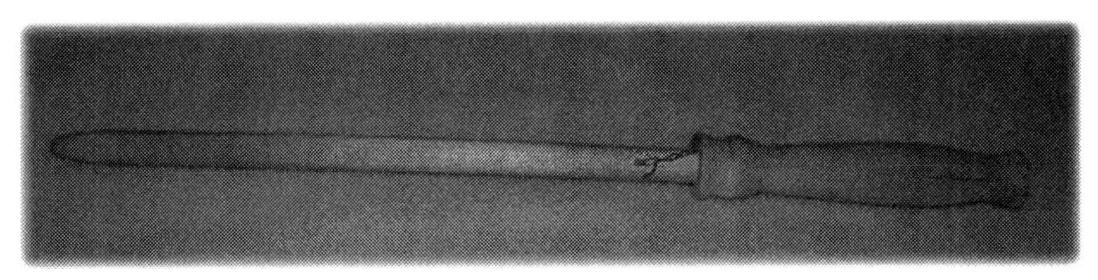

This is a Salien Pauling Wand crafted from Wych Elm. The insert is fairy hair. Note the smooth handle, a common design feature in Pauling wands.

The Verdadama (leprechauns) carry wrapped wands crafted from two complimentary woods, one for the handle and one for the wand. The wrapping is reserved for the wand itself. The wands are eight to ten inches long. The wands do not taper, they are straight from handle to tip and they end in a flat tip. The Verdadama favor leaves and vines for their wrappings. These elements, gathered and bonded to the wand while fresh, impart a greenish hue to

Verdadama wands. Verdadama wand handles are short and round, similar to the Sabedora wands. This design easily accommodates the stout hands of the Verdadama.

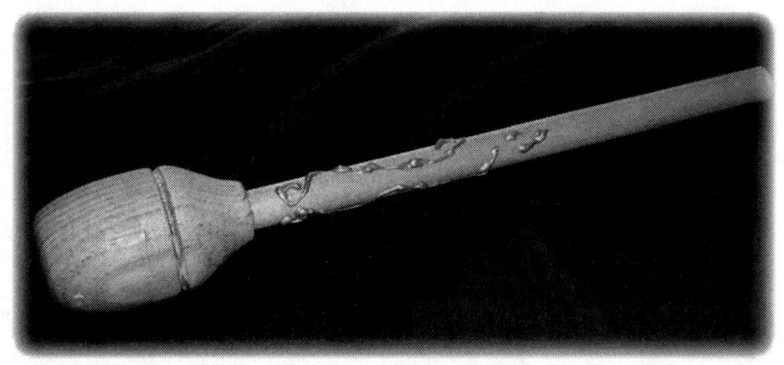

This is a Verdadama wand. Note the short, rounded handle, the round wand with the flat tip, and the wrappings on the wand itself. I made this wand for Seamus, one of the most famous Verdadama in Salien history. The wand and handle are Greenheart, the wrappings are Indian Grass.

The Eximia (giants) carry staves in the Astral style but much larger. Full grown Eximia can reach heights of around twenty-two feet tall (and some are even taller). Their staves are usually around twenty feet long and very thick. (The Eximia stave should be as wide as the Eximia's thigh – in most cases one to three feet across.) Eximia staves often have entire branches or hides wrapped around them. A few Eximia have crystals embedded in their staves as well though this is not common. The staves taper to a narrower base, usually around eight to ten inches. This is to prevent any accidental "crushing" of the wizards around the Eximia. The Eximia only carry their staves in battle or as protection. The staves themselves are fearsome weapons. Many an enemy has been crushed to death by an Eximia stave. (Eximia warriors also attach barbs to their staves – a nasty weapon indeed.)

This is an Eximia Stave. You cannot see the taper at the far end. This stave is from an oak tree. Oak is a very popular choice among the giants of the Salien for their staves. The stave is twenty feet and three inches long. It is sixteen inches in diameter at the near end.

The Evadama (wizards of human shape) carry wood wands. These handled wands are always between twelve and sixteen inches long. They are crafted from two different woods, one for the handle and one for the wand. The handles are beautifully carved. Every Evadama wand has a crystal embedded in the handle either at the base or in the middle of the handle. The crystals are created by the Elegia for the Aesir and by the Chotsir for all others. The wand is straight along the length of the shaft until it tapers to a rounded point.

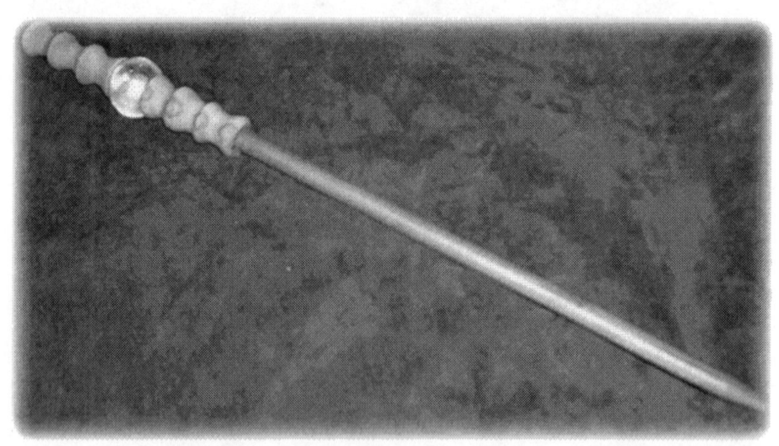

This is a Salien Evadama wand. Note the crystal embedded in the middle of the handle. Salien Evadama wands always have crystals embedded in their wands. The Wand is crafted from cherry and the handle is alder.

WANDLORE

Salien wands cover a broad range of styles, sizes, and techniques. Evadama and Elegia (elven) Wandmakers make all of the wands for the Salien with the exception of the Libertusa. (Even though the Elegia make wands, they do not use or carry wands.) Salien Wandmakers usually specialize in the technique and type of wand they make. This allows for high proficiency and output (a necessary consideration since the Salien have fought a long war). There are currently two Elegia Wandmakers and four Evadama Wandmakers who craft every type of Salien wand. One Elegia Wandmaker trained all of these generalists. It has been said by the ISW that these six Wandmakers are the greatest wandmakers the world has ever seen. The massive knowledge and skill needed to master so many different techniques is truly impressive.

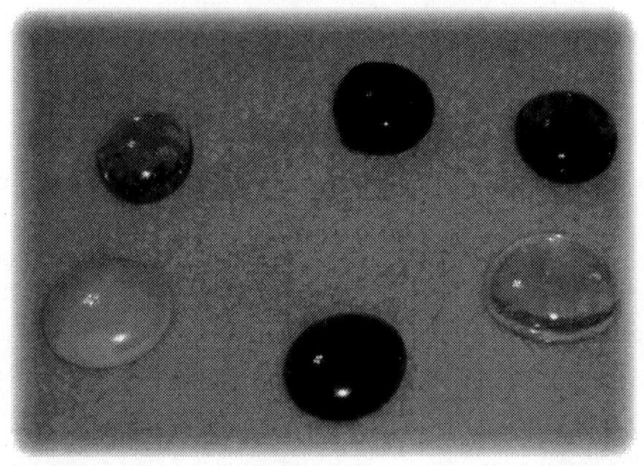

These are Elegia-made crystals for the ends of Evadama Salien wands. Note the flat bottom and rounded shape. Salien wands also may have rounded crystals or faceted crystals in the middle of the handle.

CHAPTER SEVEN

The Elements of the Wand

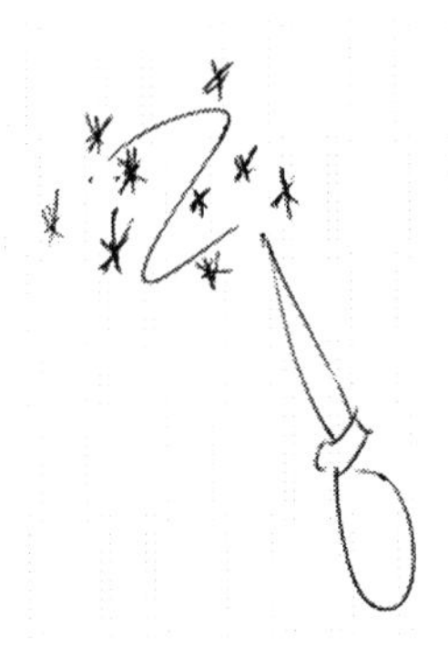

The single most important element of any wand is the wood. As I have mentioned, wand woods come from all over the world. Until the Great Journey of the Salien and especially the establishment of the ISW, Wandmakers were largely limited to native woods.

The majority of Wandmakers are very conscientious about the woods they use. More than humans, wizards are acutely cognizant of the influence they have on the natural environment. Even more importantly, many Wandmakers are friends with the nymphs, sylphs, and spirits of the trees.

A Wandmaker will never take wood from a tree without its permission. Once permission is granted, the Wandmaker may actually cut the wood. (This, of course, does not hurt the tree.) I am very aware that some humans who call themselves witches believe only fallen twigs and branches can be used for wands. This is nonsense. You must communicate with the tree and then accept the part of the tree that it has donated. On the same note, humans have also completely destroyed numerous ancient and old forests in their selfishness and greed. A Wandmaker will never use wood that has been harvested in this way. (This is part of the ISW Code of Ethics.) Wandmakers will only use wood that the tree has donated.

With the establishment of trade, many Wandmakers no longer personally gather all of the wood they use in their wands. However, all wood is gathered by Wandmakers and their apprentices. This is guaranteed by the ISW. No reputable Wandmaker will use a piece of wood unless it has the ISW seal of approval.

There are many species of wood used in wandmaking. Every species has its own strengths, weaknesses, and uses in the wand. I cannot possibly cover every species of wood, however I will give a brief description of some of the most popular and common woods and the characteristics they impart on a wand.

Wand Wood

Many wizards want to know just how they should choose the woods in their wand. (This is true for Wandmakers who adhere to the Killarney method, the Petrov method, and modern Wandmakers. Killarney Wandmakers will simply determine the best fit for you.)

There are many factors that weigh into the choice of wand woods. The general use of the wand is a primary consideration. Most wizards use one wand for all purposes but some wizard-warriors prefer to have a fighting wand in addition to their regular wand. The reason is two-fold. Having two wands allows the wizard-warrior to have a back-up in case their fighting wand breaks. The second reason is the wand-wizard bond. Wizard-warriors have reported for ages that their wands seem to pick up the intensity, anger, and some would say the "bloodlust" of battle. (It is interesting to note the early wizards always used two wands for this very reason). At first this practice (of having two wands) was limited but it is becoming much more common, especially among the Salien and the Pardologa. Both of these realms have been fighting extremely long wars.

You may ask if two wands are good, wouldn't three be better? Some wizards do have numerous wands. Each wand has a specific use (general, household, battle, school, et cetera). Some wizards also get new wands as they age. Others simply feel they have changed or their wand has changed and they are no longer a good match. There are Wandmakers who will refuse to craft more than one wand per customer while other Wandmakers are fine with the practice. The ISW does not have an official position on this practice. The ISW leaves the decision up to the individual Wandmaker.

Of course, some wizards are collectors. They have their one wand they use and merely collect other wands. This practice has been gaining in popularity. It is important to note that the "collection" wands are often very loosely bond to their owners, since they have not been used by

their owners on a regular basis.

Wizards around the world prefer different woods. Some woods gain in popularity (often due to a mention that a specific famous wizard uses a specific wood – holly and elder have been recent "fad" wood choices); rumors often fly around about the "most powerful" wand wood. This is nonsense. If you have not been paying attention, I will say it one more time. The "most powerful" wood is specific to the individual wizard. What may work for one wizard, will not work for another. So ignore the rumors, myths, and half-truths and get the wand that is best for you!

It is important to note that while each of the woods used for wands has a general magical ability. Every tree and every piece of wood has its very own characteristics in addition to its species characteristics. This is why most Wandmakers prefer to size up the wizard, assessing strengths and weaknesses, to find the perfect wand. If you would still prefer to choose your own woods, you can refer to the table at the end of this chapter for some of the magical characteristics of the most popular wand woods. I would suggest you have several choices (and the reasons you are interested in them) when you go to your

Wandmaker to order your wand. Please remember, this is a wizard with extensive knowledge of woods and elements. You should defer to their suggestions even if they differ from your own ideas.

We will take another tour around the world and cover the most common woods for each of the wizarding societies. Please refer to the tables at the end of this chapter for a quick, general reference to the various woods and elements. Also please be aware that there are, as it stands at this moment, twelve thousand, nine hundred and thirty-seven different element and wood combinations around the world currently used in the crafting of wands. Once again, your Wandmaker is the preferred source of detailed information on what is best for you.

Galdorgalere

European wood mostly comes from flowering, deciduous trees and conifers. At one point in time or another, every one of these trees has been used in wands and for wandmaking. However, not all tree species make good wands.

The most popular woods for wands used by the Galdorgalere are the alder, ash, birch, elder, hawthorn, hazel, hornbeam, holly, linden, maple, oak, pine, poplar, whitebeam (rowan), willow, wych elm, and yew. Newer native woods include beech, birch, ivy, reed, and vine.

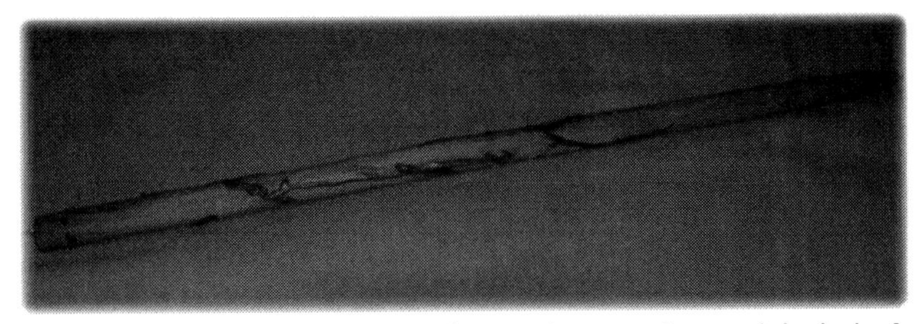

This is a modern Galdorgalere wand. Note the wrappings and the lack of a handle. The Galdorgalere, like the Salien, have readily adopted the practices of Wandmakers throughout the world. This wand has a unicorn tail insert. All Galdorgalere wands have inserts.

Sabrils

As noted previously, the Sabrils of Asia primarily used cypress in their wands. In most areas of the world, cypress is the Wood of Life (or long-life depending on the interpretation). Cypress does not necessarily bring a long life to the wizard who wields it but Sabril wands are known for the endurance of the spells cast by them.

Modern Sabril wands use woods from all over the world. Popular choices among Sabril Wandmakers today are almond, ash, bamboo, larch, maple, oak, poplar, and wormwood. The Sabrils have also begun importing ebony, cherry, and redheart for use in their wands.

Astrals

Eucalyptus is by far the most common wood used in Astral staves, especially by younger Astrals. Eucalyptus has strong, protective properties. Other popular choices for Astral staves are ash, beech, cedar, oak, and spruce.

Pardaloga

Early Pardaloga Wands were made from crystals but wood was eventually incorporated into the wands. Cypress was the most popular wood for wand handles. The cypress was traded to the Pardaloga by the Sabrils. Popular woods in

WANDLORE

Pardaloga wands are teak, palm, asoka, nim, and spruce.

Kibojara

Africa is home to some of the most diverse species of wand woods. Popular wand woods include ebony, pink ivory (a pink wood related to ebony), yellowheart, teak, sandalwood, rosewood, purpleheart, bloodwood, zebrawood, lacewood, and acacia.

Sabedora

Like Africa, South America has many species of wand wood. Some of these commonly used in wands around the world are acacia, jacarada, mahogany, pine, mangrove, palm, greenheart, and walnut.

Salien

North America has an abundant supply of deciduous and conifer trees, as well as some sub-tropical species. Native North American woods commonly used in wands

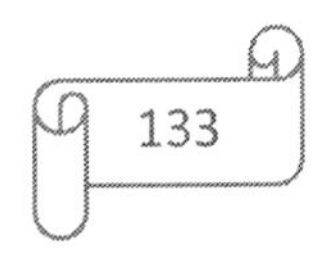

include ash, birch, elm, cherry, chestnut, cottonwood, dogwood, hickory, apple, oak, willow, pine, poplar, redwood, and hazel.

TABLE 1 – WOODS USED IN WANDMAKING AROUND THE WORLD

WOOD	STRENGTHS	GOOD MATCHES	CONFLICTS	SPECIAL NOTES
Acacia	Excellent for defensive spells	Eucalyptus, Almond	Birch, Orange	Acacia is popular with the Sabedora.
Alder	Overall wand wood good for spells and charms	Orange, Chestnut	Wych Elm, Apple	Alder is one of the classic wand woods.
Almond	Adds toughness to your wand	Acacia, Mahogany	Worm-wood, Willow	Almond is very hard.
Apple	Adds longevity to your wand	Chestnut, Cottonwood	Acacia, Wych Elm	Apple is the symbol of immortality.
Ash	Ash is a protective wood. Good for defensive spells.	Walnut, Chestnut	Birch, Lacewood	Kibojara warriors use ash in their wands.

WANDLORE

Asoka	Adds resolve to your wand	Bamboo, Acacia	Cherry, Chestnut	Good for casting spells
Bamboo	Adds a quickness to your wand	Eucalyptus, Poplar	Walnut, Jacarada	Unlike most woods, bamboo is protected by xanas and not nymphs.
Beech	Adds spirit to your wand	Apple, Hawthorn	Ash, Hazel	Beech is a preferred wood for wizards who have trouble remember-ing spells.
Birch	Adds resilience to your wand	Poplar, Larch	Acacia, Ash	The most popular wood for broomsticks
Bloodwood	Adds brilliance to your wand	Hazel, Holly	Redheart, Redwood	Bloodwood is a deep red color.
Cedar	Good for defensive spells.	Wych Elm, Hawthorn	Redwood, Cherry	Cedar has long-lasting protective qualities.
Cherry	Adds radiance to your wand	Apple, Dogwood	Asoka, Laurel	Cherry is a popular part of love potions.

Chestnut	Adds strength to your wand	Ash, Alder	Mahogany Rosewood	Chestnut is often used by the Libertusa in their wands.
Cottonwood	Adds toughness to your wand	Redwood, Cedar	Bamboo, Eucalyptus	Cottonwood is very hardy.
Cypress	Adds power and endurance to your wand	Most woods	Yew, Lignum Vitae	The Wood of Life
Dogwood	Adds resolve to your wand	Apple, Lacewood	Ebony, Eucalyptus	Very popular in old Mellas staves.
Ebony	The Wood of Power (but very incompat-ible with many woods.)	Bloodwood, beech, hornbeam, elm, redheart, rowan, and wormwood.	All other woods but especially cypress, holly, lignum vitae, and yew	Ebony is a powerful wood but it can only be used with the woods listed.
Elder	A classic, powerful wand wood.	Hawthorn, Wych Elm	Linden, Cedar	Elder can be very powerful when paired with the right woods.

WANDLORE

Elm				See the entry for Wych Elm
Eucalyptus	Very strong protective properties	Acacia, Lignum Vitae	Dogwood, Cedar	The most popular wood for Astral staves.
Greenheart	A high caliber wand wood.	Willow, Laurel	Lacewood, Olive	Greenheart is the favored wand wood among the Verdadama.
Hawthorn	Sharpens the powers of your wand	Elder, Almond	Larch, Pine	Hawthorn is one of the three fairy trees.
Hazel	A classic, overall wand wood good for spells and charms	Greenheart, Almond	Alder, Holly	Hazel is one of the most popular wand woods.
Holly	Very strong protective powers – excellent in anti-Dark spells	Bloodwood, Olive	Yew, Worm-wood	Gaining in popularity around the world as a classic wand wood.

Hornbeam	A strong, tough wood. Good for defensive spells.	Almond, Dogwood	Linden, Mahogany	A popular wood in eastern Europe and England
Ivy	See the entry for Greenheart			All ivy used in wands is greenheart.
Jacarada	Adds resilience to your wand	Pine, Palm	Alder, Bamboo	Jacarada has strong healing properties.
Lacewood	Adds crispness to your wand	Larch, Hazel	Ash, Greenheart	Lacewood is a favorite of the Kibojara.
Larch	Excellent wood for dragon wranglers	Birch, Lacewood	Hazel, Spruce	Larch cannot be penetrated by magical or creature fires.
Laurel	A springy wand wood	Greenheart, Birch	Cherry, Hawthorn	Some Wand-makers will only use laurel donated in the springtime for wands.

Lignum Vitae	Has some longevity capabilities but is really only an adequate wand wood, not stellar	Orange, Almond	Olive, Cypress	Translates from Latin to "Wood of Life" but not as strong as Cypress.
Linden	Good protective qualities	Greenheart, Laurel	Elder, Hornbeam	Popular with the Galdorgalere and Pardaloga
Mahogany	Adds stability to your wand	Holly, Almond	Rosewood, Hornbeam	Mahogany is favored by the Kibojara.
Makore	Adds fortitude to your wand	Mahogany, Poplar	Maple, Oak	Popular with the Sabedora
Mangrove	Adds brilliance to your wand	Orange, Nim	Pink Ivory, Oak	Popular with the Pardaloga
Maple	Adds resilience to your wand	Pine, Whitebeam	Makore, Nim	Maple is one of the earliest woods used in wands by the Salien.

Nim	Adds resolve to your wand	Palm, Mangrove	Birch, Alder	Often paired with palm in warrior wands.
Oak	The strongest of wand woods.	Hazel, Willow	Walnut, Reed	Eximia staves are often made from oak.
Olive	Adds potency to your wand	Holly, Almond	Lignum vitae, Yew	Olive is a sacred tree to the Elegia.
Orange	Adds springiness to your wand	Alder, Lignum Vitae	Yellow-heart, Redheart	Orange is a popular ingredient in numerous potions.
Palm	Palm has protective properties.	Orange, Jacarada	Pine, Birch	Palm is particularly effective against evil creatures and monsters
Pine	A very strong protective wood	Maple, Jacarada	Acacia, Hawthorn	Popular among warriors
Pink Ivory	Strong with spells especially in the hands of female wizards	Whitebeam, Tuilipwood	Mangrove, Nim, Ebony	Popular with female wizards. Will not work in conjunction with ebony.

WANDLORE

Poplar	Adds resilience to your wand	Birch, Maple	White-beam, Holly	Poplar is the second most popular wood for broomsticks.
Purpleheart	Good healing properties	Pink Ivory, Alder	Redwood, Bloodwood	An excellent partner for pink ivory.
Redheart	Adds fortitude to your wand	Whitebeam, Spruce	Bloodwood Cedar	Redheart is popular among the Pumilla.
Redwood	Strong, tough wood second only to oak.	Poplar, Cottonwood	Purple-heart, Rosewood	Popular with the Salien, especially the Libertusa and the Eximia.
Reed				See the entry for bamboo
Rowan				See the entry for Whitebeam
Rosewood	Adds radiance to your wand	Willow, Birch	Purple-heart, Hornbeam	Rosewood has a nice, crisp feel.
Sandalwood	Adds brightness to your wand	Teak, Cypress	Walnut, Orange	Sandalwood is the second most popular wood in Sabril wands.

Spruce	Adds toughness to your wand	Redheart, Yellowheart	Larch, Birch	Popular among the Eximia for their staves
Teak	Adds durability to your wand	Sandalwood Pine	Oak, Apple	Teak is popular with the Pardologa and the Kibojara.
Tulipwood	Adds potency to your wand	Pink Ivory, Whitebeam	Wormwoo dYellow-heart	Tulipwood also has strong protective properties.
Vine				See the entry for rosewood
Walnut	Adds strength to your wand	Beech, Ash	Reed, Rosewood	Walnut is a very loyal wood.
Whitebeam (Rowan)	The classic, overall wand wood.	Walnut, Sandalwood	Poplar, Cotton-wood	One of the most common wand woods used worldwide.
Willow	Strong healing properties.	Elder, Alder	Almond, Linden	Excellent wood for spells and charms.

WANDLORE

Wormwood	Preferred for silent spells.	Ebony, Willow	Yellow-heart, Wych Elm	Popular with Samjas (wizards who seek out and destroy dark wizards).
Wych Elm	Adds toughness to your wand	Elder, Mahogany	Apple, Worm-wood	The Elegia often work with elm.
Yellowheart	Adds brightness to your wand	Ash, Spruce	Orange, cedar	Yellowheart is said to enhance courage.
Yew	Yew is a very powerful wand wood, good for dark spells and defense against dark spells. Popular with warriors.	Yew does not work well with any other wood in particular …	… cypress, ebony, olive, and holly	Yew is the "Wood of Death" – so named for its human uses in bows and coffins.
Zebrawood	Strong protective and offensive powers	Whitebeam, mahogany	Cypress, Olive	Zebrawood can be tempera-mental in wands.

Elements

Wand elements cover a wide range of plants, flowers, vines, and leaves as well as magical creature elements, crystals, jewels, and metals. Every one of these elements adds a characteristic to the wand. Some elements are only used in their native land, others are common worldwide.

Many Wandmakers around the world use elements in their wands. At one time or another, Wandmakers have tried using parts of every magical creature. Most elements were incompatible with wandmaking. As a result, the number of creatures suitable for wandmaking is limited. In general, Wandmakers have found mostly non-speaking creatures are good sources for wand elements (with a few notable exceptions). Most Wandmakers have limited the creature elements to fur, hair, whiskers, barbs, scales, and feathers.

Some elements are completely incompatible with wands. Blood cannot be used in wands, for instance. Wandmakers have tried using the blood from salamanders, dragons, basilisk, and gryphons without success. In all cases, the blood made the wand unworkable - no spells, curses, or charms would work. Consequently, modern Wandmakers do not use any blood or blood products in wands.

Other magical creature elements that have proven completely unsuitable to wands are poisons and venoms. Once again, these elements render the wand unusable. Generally, Wandmakers have found creature elements that can be donated willingly by the creature work the best.

The most commonly used magical creature elements are tail hairs from unicorns and centaurs, fur from sidhe and gryphons, feathers from hippogriffs, phoenixes, firgara, hamsa, muninn, and raicho, scales from salamanders, dragons, and mermaids, hair from pixies, vilas, fairies, and xanas, and roc horn powder. Of all of the magical creatures who provide elements for wands, the dragon is by far the most versatile. In addition to scales, dragons provide whiskers, tail barbs, and (by the Galdorgalere only) heartstrings all of which are used in wands around the world. Fairies, pixies, centaurs, vilas, mermaids, xanas, and some gryphon are, of course, speaking creatures. They must willingly donate the elements that are used in wands. In addition, firgara, phoenix, roc, hamsa, and raicho must willingly donate the feathers and horns used for Wandmaking. (Some Wandmakers will use discarded feathers and horns or feathers found in nests. This is a controversial practice as the feathers still belong to the creature. As you are aware, these feathers are extremely valuable and in the case of the firgara, raicho, and phoenix the feathers, if properly hatched, create new creatures. This is why donation is so important. We are, in essence, taking the potential offspring of these creatures to be used in our wands. The ISW is close to banning the practice of raiding nests, a move applauded by nearly all Wandmakers.)

Elements from common animals have been tried (owl feathers and cat hair are the two most common) but they do not work in wands. They do not affect the wand at all and are considered inert by Wandmakers.

TABLE TWO – MAGICAL CREATURE INSERTS

MAGICAL CREA-TURE	ELEMENT	STRENGTHS	GOOD MATCHES	CONFLICTS	SPECIAL NOTES
Centaur	Tail Hair	Adds nobility to your wand	Vila	Mermaid	The Centaurs of Australia and America donate the most tail hair for wand use.
Dragon	Scales	Adds durability to your wand	Sala-mander	Fairies, Xanas	Dragon scales are plentiful.
	Barbs	Adds "zing" to your wand	Sala-mander	Fairies, Xanas	Barbs are the newest elements used in wands.
	Whiskers	Adds agility to your wand	Salaman-der	Fairies, Xanas	More potent than heartstrings
	Heart-strings	No known benefit – whiskers are better		Not used in conjunct-tion with any other elements.	Only used by the Galdor-galere.
Fairy	Hair	Adds lumin-escence to your wand	Xanas	Dragon, Pixie	Fairy hairs are extremely fine.

Firgara	Feather	Adds spirit to your wand	Sala-mander	Phoenix, Raicho	Firgara feathers are very difficult, and dangerous, to collect.
Gryphon	Fur	Adds ferocity to your wand	Sidhe	Hippo-griff, Mermaid	The fur can only be collected from the limited number of tame Gryhons.
Hamsa	Feather	Adds longevity to your wand	Hippo-griff	Dragon	Hamsa are immortal.
Hippo-griff	Feather	Adds keenness to your wand	Hamsa	Gryphon	Hippogriffs have the best eyesight of any magical creature.
Mermaid	Scale	Adds fierceness to your wand	Dragon	Vila, Gryphon	Mermaids must donate their scales.
Muninn	Feather	Adds briskness to your wand	Pixies	Roc, Firgara	Muninn feathers are black.

WANDLORE

Phoenix	Feather	Adds intensity to your wand	None known	Does not work well with any other elements	The Phoenix is the most intelligent and powerful of the non-speaking magical creatures.
Pixies	Hair	Adds liveliness to your wand	Muninn	Raicho, Fairie	Pixie hair can be difficult to use in wands.
Raicho	Feather	Adds firmness to your wand	Roc	Muninn	The song of the Raicho can deafen all enemies for one hundred miles.
Roc	Horn	Adds resilience to your wand	Firgara	Muninn	The Roc is a great, horned bird found only in the Americas.
Salamander	Scales	Adds brilliance to your wand	Dragon	Vila	Salamander scales can only be picked up using dragon scale gloves – they will melt everything else.

Sidhe	Fur	Adds stability to your wand	Gryphon	Dragon	The Sidhe is sacred to the Pardaloga.
Unicorn	Tail Hair	Adds soundness to your wand	Mermaid Centaur	Vila	Unicorns are one the most intelligent, non-speaking magical creatures.
Vila	Hair	Adds a capricious-ness to your wand	Centaur	Pixies, Mermaids	Vila hairs are very tempera-mental.
Xanas	Hair	Adds buoyancy to your wand	Fairies	Dragon	Xanas are water-spirits who protect woodland streams and lakes.

Plant elements are also common in many wands around the world. There are literally thousands of plants, magical and common, which have been tried in wands. These are rarely used as inserts, the more common application is wrappings (or in the case of the Kibojara as

essences and as a part of the crystal by the Chotsir). Once again, Wandmakers have perfected the best plant elements for wands. Not all plants work well in wandmaking. Fortunately, most Wandmakers have a complete listing of every wand they have ever made. This has allowed the ISW to cross-reference these records and publish a list of Preferred Plant Elements. This list is reproduced here (for the first time to non-Wandmakers). It should be noted that the Galdorgalere have only recently begun to use plant elements in their wands and have not explored the abundance of their native plants and their effects on wands. The ISW is conducting experiments and expects to add Galdorgalere plant elements to their preferred list in the future.

TABLE THREE – MAGICAL PLANTS USED IN WANDMAKING

PLANTS	STRENGTHS	GOOD MATCHES	CONFLICT	SPECIAL NOTES
Antigonon	Adds rigidness to your wand	Hippogriff Feathers	Hamsa Feathers	Favored by the Sabedora
Bougain-villea	Adds changeability to your wand	Salamander Scales	Bougainvillea conflicts with all other plant elements	Bougainvilla is very temper-amental

Calamint	Adds calmness to your wand	Roc Horn	Dragon elements	Calamint is a favorite of the Verdadama
Crimson Waratah	Adds flare to your wand	Dragon Scales	Roc Horn	Favored by Astrals
Flame of the Forest	Adds spark to your wand	Salamander scales, xanas hair	Vila Hair, Pixie Hair	Favored by the Chotsir and the Astrals
Gardenia	Adds sweetness to your wand	Vila Hair	Mermaid Scales	Used by the Sabrils
Golden Champah	Adds lightness to your wand	Raicho Feathers, Sidhe Fur	Vila Hair	Favored by Sabrils
Goldthread	Adds heartiness to your wand	Unicorn Tail Hair	Sidhe Fur	A deep, golden color that accents many wand woods
Golden Red Banksias	Adds passion to your wand	Gryphon Fur	Vila Hair	Favored by Astrals
Ixoro	Adds springiness to your wand	Dragon Whiskers	Hippogriff Feathers	Common on Sabril wands

WANDLORE

Indian Grass	Adds flexibility to your wand	Gryphon Fur, Roc Horn	Salamander Scales	First used in Mellas Staves, a popular element worldwide
Lantana	Adds steadiness to your wand	Vila Hair, Mermaid Scales	Unicorn Tail Hair	Favored by the Sabedora
Lilium	Adds durability to your wand	Mermaid Scales	Dragon Scales	Lilium is a common potion ingredient
Moonbeam	Adds potency to your wand	Phoenix Feathers	Muninn Feathers	Moonbeam is the only element that can in conjunction with Phoenix Feathers
Obavata	Adds hardness to your wand	Muninn Feathers	Pixie Hair	The berries of this plant are commonly used in wands and in potions.
Paintbrush	Adds firmness to your wand	Hippogriff Feathers	Gryphon Fur	Paintbrush is a popular element in warrior wands.

Quisqualis	Adds suppleness to your wand	Sidhe Fur	Xanas Hair	A Sabedora plant element
Red Silk Cotton	Adds staunchness to your wand	Pixie Hair	Dragon Barbs	Red Silk Cotton flowers are often used in love potions.
Scarlet Firewheel	Adds brilliance to your wand	Roc Horns	Muninn Feathers	Used by the Astrals
Shivalin-gara	Adds resilience to your wand	Dragon Barbs	Dragon Whiskers	Used by the Pardaloga

Other elements used in wands are crystals, jewels, and, less frequently, metals. I cannot say much about the crystals and jewels used in wands due to the fact that the Chotsir and the Elegia were not willing to divulge this information. However, I have been permitted to list the accepted powers of these elements relative to color only. Please see the chart below.

TABLE FOUR – CRYSTAL COLORS USED IN WANDS

CRYSTAL COLOR	STRENGTHS	MATCHES	CONFLICTS	SPECIAL NOTES
Black	Adds fortitude to your wand	Centaur Tail Hair	Hamsa Feathers	Black is a common choice in warrior wands.
Blue	Adds wisdom to your wand	Hamsa Feathers	Sidhe Fur	Sapphires are the Stone of Destiny.
Clear	Adds clarity to your wand	Good with all other elements		The Chotsir make fine, faceted, clear crystals used worldwide.
Gold	Adds strength to your wand	Unicorn Tail hair	Mermaid Scales	Amber is a popular choice for gold crystals
Green	Adds firmness to your wand	Mermaid Scales	Pixie Hair	Emerald is the Stone of Wisdom.

Purple	Adds regality to your wand	Dragon Barbs	Salaman-der Scales	Amethysts are the Stone of Royalty
Red	Adds power to your wand	Roc Horn	Pixie Hair	Rubies are the Stone of Kings
White	Adds pureness to your wand	Moon-beam	Roc Horn	Moonstone is the most popular white stone used in wands.

The metals used in Wandmaking are almost all made by the Elegia or Libertusa. Neither would divulge any details of these metals.

It is important to note I have only provided the briefest of descriptions for these elements. You must depend on the knowledge of your Wandmaker to optimize the elements for you.

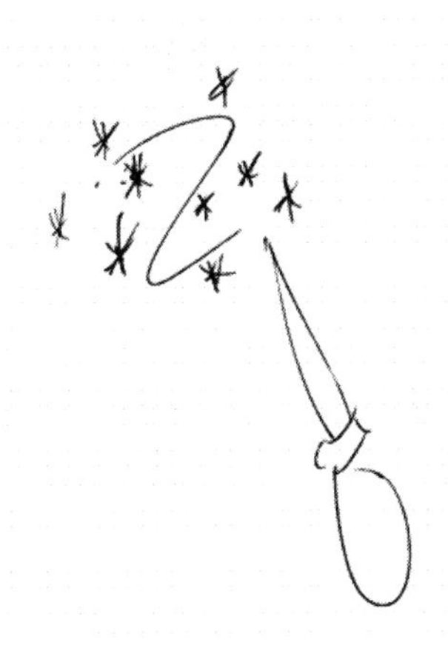

A Final Word

As you can see, the world of wands and wandmaking is diverse and extensive, so much so that this book has only scratched the surface of the knowledge and history of this wondrous object. Whether the wand finds the wizard or the wizard chooses the wand is, in the end, the least important of the mysteries and secrets of wands. For the true secret lies in the life the wand leads with its wizard.

PRINCIPLES OF WIZARDRY
VOLUME ONE

Wandmakers have long known the knowledge they have today is only a pittance of the knowledge they will have in a year, ten years, or a lifetime of Wandmaking. While we may have unlocked some of the secrets of the wand, we, as Wandmakers, know there are an uncountable and unfathomable number of secrets we still must learn. As a Wandmaker I can assure you of this one truth: The relationship between the wand, the wizard, and the Wandmaker is dynamic and fluid - just like the art, the craft, the science, and the study of Wandlore.

WANDLORE

WANDLORE

Power and Practice

A Complete Guide to the Wizard Wand

by

The Wandmaker and Annette M Musta

To order more copies of this book, please visit us at:

www.arhbooks.com

This book is distributed through Baker & Taylor

Wholesale discounts available directly from the publisher

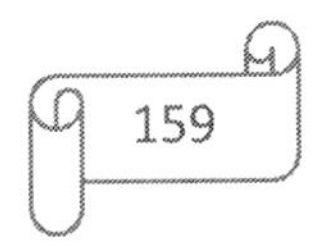